SURRENDER TO LOVE

A Novella

by

MaryAnn Diorio

TopNotch Press
A Division of MaryAnn Diorio Enterprises, LLC
Merchantville, NJ 08109

SURRENDER TO LOVE
by MaryAnn Diorio
Published by TopNotch Press
A Division of MaryAnn Diorio Enterprises, LLC
PO Box 1185
Merchantville, NJ 08109

Unless otherwise indicated, all Scripture quotations are from the ESV® Bible by Crossway, a publishing ministry of Good News Publishers. Used by permission. All rights reserved.

Library of Congress Control Number: 2015909367

ISBN: 978-0-930037-25-3 Publisher's Note: This is a work of fiction. Names, characters, places, and incidents are either the product of the author's imagination or are used fictitiously, and any resemblance to actual persons, living or dead, businesses, companies, events, or locales is entirely coincidental.

While the author has made every effort to provide accurate telephone numbers and Internet addresses at the time of publication, neither the publisher nor the author assumes any responsibility for errors or for changes that occur after publication. Further, the publisher and author do not have any control over and do not assume any responsibility for author or third-party websites or their content.

Cover Design by Lynette Sowell
Cover Photo: Fotolia.com File: #81108840 | Author: littleny

Praise for the Fiction of MaryAnn Diorio

A Christmas Homecoming
Winner of the Silver Medal for E-Book Fiction in the 2015 Illumination Book Awards sponsored by the Jerry Jenkins Group

"This short story is a wonderful way to start the Christmas season. It is a story full of human emotion and the struggles this life can challenge us with. The lesson throughout the story is that all things are possible through God's grace. This is a 'feel good' story that lifts the spirits and keeps you encouraging the main character to persevere and not give up. It is a great book for a short respite from our busy lives." ~ *Kimberly T. Ferland, Amazon.com*

"Well-woven. If only all stories made me sit on the edge of my seat, unsure of the outcome, but desperate for a good conclusion for the characters!" ~ *Sarah E. Johnson, Poet, Amazon.com*

"A great Christian read. A powerful short story packed full of love, hope, heartbreak and a strong message on forgiveness." ~ *Jerron, Amazon.com*

Do Angels Ride Ponies?
Children's chapter book for 8-12-year-olds

"The story is beautiful, and I found myself emotionally touched by it. Tears filled my eyes at the ending. I also loved the message that this book sends, that anything is possible if we believe. I would recommend this book to anyone, from any walk of faith and any age. This book is filled with compassion, and the Biblical phrase, 'Anything is possible if a person believes,' is easily one of the most powerful and truthful statements of all time." ~ *Stefani Milanese, Author and Hostess of "Read All About It," RadioVision Network*

"I read Dr. Diorio's book to my 6 year old son, Gabriel. He really loved the story and told me so all the way through. The story was so interesting that I could not put it down. We finished it in one sitting. We learned that anything is possible with God. . . .This book inspires me to reach for my dreams. I loved it!" ~ *Vicki Oswald, Author*

"I truly enjoyed this book and the message it conveys to the children who will read it. *Do Angels Ride Ponies?* not only teaches the truth of God's Word, but also the potential each one of us has when we believe and act on that truth." ~ *Deborah Piccurelli, Author of Hush, Little Baby*

ACKNOWLEDGMENTS

A book is a joint venture, put together with the help of many people. I would like to thank those who worked closely with me on this story, from the brainstorming stage, through the writing stage, and, finally, through the editing stage.

First of all, I would like to thank my God and Father Who gave me both the gift to write and the desire to exercise that gift for His glory. I would like to thank my Lord and Savior Jesus Christ who first gave me the idea for this story, and I would like to thank Holy Spirit for hovering over me with His wisdom and understanding as I wrote this story.

Next, I would like to thank my amazing husband of 45 years, Dominic A. Diorio, MD, who encouraged me along the way and helped me practically by cooking meals and cleaning the house while I worked to meet deadlines.

Special thanks go to my daughters, Lia Diorio Gerken, Ph.D., and Gina L. Diorio, M.A., an outstanding writer in her own right, who continually support me with their love and prayers.

Last, but certainly not least, I would like to thank my wonderful fiction writing colleagues, editors, and dear sisters in Christ—Rose Allen McCauley, Lynette Sowell, and Vasthi Acosta—who offered valuable assistance and served as astute critique partners and content editors. Your valuable insights served to make this story so much better.

Finally, I would like to thank all of you who read this story. May it bless you and touch you with the love of Christ. May you experience the great joy that comes from complete surrender to His endless love for you.

DEDICATION

To my Lord and Savior Jesus Christ . . .

In Whom I live and move and have my being . . .

Thank You for giving me stories that transform hearts
for You.

Glory to Your Holy Name forevermore!

SURRENDER TO LOVE

"For my thoughts are not your thoughts,
neither are your ways my ways, declares the LORD."

Isaiah 55: 8 ESV

Table of Contents

AUTHOR'S NOTE

In Matthew 16:25, Jesus said this: "If you try to hang on to your life, you will lose it. But if you give up your life for my sake, you will save it."

Years ago, I was trying to hang on to my life. I had been in a doctoral program for nearly seven years and was only three months from graduating when I heard Holy Spirit speak to my heart: "Will you give up your PhD for Me?" At first the thought seemed crazy. Give up seven years of hard work? Give up something for which I'd prepared for my entire educational career?

Give up my dream?

As I prayed and sought God, the words kept penetrating my heart. "Will you give up your PhD for Me?'

After prayer and seeking God, I bowed to His will and gave up my PhD. My professors thought I had lost my mind, that, perhaps, all the studying had gotten to my brain. But I knew in my heart that I was obeying God, even though I did not understand Him.

Instantly, I felt perfect peace. For the next several months, I ministered to God's people in the ways He led. Then, I heard His voice again. "Finish your PhD."

"Lord, is that You?" I asked.

"Yes, dear one. You have proven to Me that You love Me more than your PhD. You have surrendered your life to Me. Now the PhD will not keep you from Me. It will be My instrument to lead others to Me."

And so, I completed my doctoral program.

To follow Christ means to be willing to surrender everything to Him. In the story you are about to read, the main character struggles to let go of something that is very dear to her heart and that is keeping her from total surrender to the will of God for her life, much as I had done with my PhD.

Perhaps you, too, are struggling to let go of something that is keeping you from surrendering to God's will for your life. If you are in such a struggle, my prayer is that, as you read this story, you will come to know that true freedom lies in losing our lives for Christ's sake. You will never be truly free until you are ready to die to yourself and live totally for Jesus Christ.

Dr. MaryAnn Diorio
June 17, 2015
Merchantville, New Jersey

Surrender to Love

Prologue

Dr. Teresa Lopez Gonzalez screamed, stumbled, and stifled a sob with her fist. "No! It's not true!" She gasped for air as the tragic news sucked the life out of her. "You're talking about the wrong person. It can't be my husband. Roberto is at work."

Trembling, she grabbed the edge of the kitchen counter to keep from falling.

This couldn't be happening to her. Surely it was all a dream. A bad dream. She would awaken soon to discover all was well.

The police officer lowered his head then lifted it again. Compassion filled his glistening eyes. "Ma'am. I'm sorry. So very sorry." He reached into his belt pouch. "We found this in your husband's shirt pocket."

Teresa's stomach clenched. She immediately recognized the blue identification badge that Roberto carried to his job five days a week as chief mural artist for the city of New York. He'd been so proud of his current project—an outdoor mural for the north wall of the Drug Rehabilitation Building in Harlem. An attempt to revitalize the neighborhood where he volunteered in his spare time to minister to street gangs. He'd been thrilled to get the assignment.

Dizziness coiled itself around her brain, strangling her thinking. Her body shook with cold tremors as her mind spun deliriously.

1

She could still hear her husband's voice lingering in her ear from their parting conversation that morning. "I love you, Tessa Babe." Her chest clenched. He always called her by her nickname. "I'll be thinking of you today. Can't wait to get home to you tonight."

Teresa stumbled back as a wrenching sob overtook her.

The officer handed her the ID.

Her hands shook as she reached for the familiar badge. Roberto's handsome face looked at her with that warm smile she'd grown to love so much during their two, oh-so-short years of marriage. Another sob formed in her throat, stifling her breath. She shook her head. Impossible. Roberto could not be dead. Just this morning she'd kissed him goodbye with all the passion of their first love and an expectation that he'd be home after work.

But now he would never come home again.

Never.

Dazed, she fell into the nearest chair and stared through the window of the kitchen door behind the officer. A light rain fell against a gray sky. "What happened?" Her voice was barely a whisper. "Please, tell me what happened?"

The officer plunged his thumbs into his belt. "The scaffold collapsed, and your husband fell."

Teresa cringed as waves of nausea convulsed her. She looked up at the officer's face, grim with concern. "My husband was painting a mural on the old drug rehab building in Harlem. He was working outside the ninth floor." The words caught in her throat.

The officer nodded, anguish written all over his face. "Our investigation showed that the scaffold had not been properly secured and—"

She raised an open palm and shook her head. "No more. Please. Don't tell me anymore." The horrific image of Roberto hurtling to the ground was more than she could bear. What were his final thoughts? Did he even have time to think? He was ready to die, she knew that. But he wouldn't want to die in such a horrific way.

"I understand, ma'am. Is there anything I can do for you?"

Fire welled up in her throat. "No. Nothing. Thank you for doing your job."

"Sorry to have been the harbinger of bad news, ma'am." He gave her a nod of respect, opened the back door, and left.

Yielding to the gut-wrenching sobs that exploded from her soul, Teresa buried her face in her hands and wept.

Chapter One

Five years later . . .

Arms laden with the day's mail, Teresa fumbled in her purse for the key to the apartment she shared with her widowed mother Marisol. Teresa looked forward to relaxing after a grueling day at the life coaching center. Even though home was now Mamá's apartment. After Roberto's untimely death, Teresa had accepted her mother's generous invitation to move in with her. According to Mamá, two widows living in the same house were better than one. Especially since those widows were mother and daughter.

But Teresa had her doubts. Had Roberto not left her with only a small insurance policy, she would have preferred to live on her own. At least she'd had enough money to complete her advanced degree in life coaching, something she'd wanted to do for a long time. With that sheepskin in hand, her options had dramatically increased, as had her income. Once she built her coaching practice to where she wanted it, she'd move out and get a place of her own.

Teresa located the key just as Mamá opened the door.

"I saw you through the window." Mamá embraced her daughter. "Come in from the cold. December in New Jersey feels like the North Pole."

Teresa rolled her eyes. "How do you know, Mamá? You've never been to the North Pole."

Mamá laughed. "Cold is cold no matter where you

find it. Ah, for the warm climate of Puerto Rico." Mamá rubbed her hands.

Teresa entered the apartment and shut the door against the frigid wind behind her. She suppressed a wave of shivers. "A warmer climate does sound more inviting right about now." Teresa gave Mamá a peck on the cheek. "So, how was your day?"

"The usual. Bible study. Prayer. Then grocery shopping for today's meals." Mamá smiled. "I made your favorite. *Arroz con pollo*."

"Thank you." Mamá meant well, but returning to live with her mother had not been easy. For one thing, Mamá controlled the menu. Sometimes, when Teresa got home from work, all she wanted to do was order pizza or make a sandwich. But Mamá always had a hot meal prepared for her.

While Mamá dished out the evening meal, Teresa sorted through the mail. The usual. Junk flyers and a few bills. She laid the bills to one side and gathered the advertisements. She was about to throw them into the trashcan when a small yellow envelope slid out from the pile of flyers. It was addressed to Mamá from Ramona Sanchez, Mamá's childhood friend in Puerto Rico.

"You must be hungry." Mamá set the plates on the kitchen table.

"Smells good, but I'm not very hungry. "

Mamá straightened and furrowed her brows. "Teresa Rosita, you must start eating more." When Mamá wanted to make a point, she always called her by her full given name. "Ever since Roberto died, you've become as thin as an *habichuela verde*."

Teresa stiffened. "I am not as thin as a green bean, Mamá."

The older woman pointed a finger in warning. "Well, you are close to it. And you, a doctor. You should know better."

"I'm a doctor of philosophy."

Mamá shook her finger. "That's even more reason for you to practice good sense. Philosophy is about loving wisdom, isn't it? And good philosophy means thinking wisely, doesn't it? And thinking wisely means eating enough to take care of your body, right?"

Teresa blew out a long breath. She couldn't deny her mother's simple logic, although it didn't quite fit in with her own understanding of philosophy. She stifled a smile and handed the yellow envelope to Mamá. "For you. From Ramona."

Mamá took the envelope and turned it over, inspecting the stamp. She carefully opened the flap. "This must be her annual Christmas update." Mamá opened the envelope. "So, it's not her Christmas letter. It's a personal letter." She read it aloud.

Teresa listened while removing her coat and scarf. Ramona's son Marcos was having trouble with his thirteen-year-old daughter Pilar. Teresa vaguely remembered her mother's telling her, several years earlier, about Ramona's granddaughter whose mother had died in childbirth. Teresa's heart tightened. Poor girl. No wonder she was having challenges.

Her mother continued to read. "Since your daughter Teresa is a life coach, my son Marcos would like to hire her to coach Pilar. He thinks coaching will give Pilar some goals and help her move on with her life. Do you think Teresa would be willing to come to Puerto Rico for a short visit?"

Mamá looked up and smiled. "Teresa, this would be perfect for you. You could get away for a while to deal with your own troubled heart and, at the same time, you could help Ramona's granddaughter."

Teresa clenched her jaw. Once again Mamá was trying to plan her life for her. "Mamá, I can't get away right now. I can't afford it. Besides, I have clients I have to take care of here in the States."

Her mother put an arm around her and smiled sheepishly. "You worry too much. I was planning to give you a vacation trip as a Christmas gift. God knows you need a vacation. And what better place to go than Puerto Rico?" Mamá gave her a smug look. "So the travel expense problem is solved."

Teresa couldn't do this. She couldn't leave her hometown. The town where she'd lived with Roberto. The town where he was buried. Who would put Christmas flowers on his grave? Who would weep for him?

Who would uphold his memory? A memory she wore like a badge of honor.

To betray that memory in any way would be to betray the man she'd adored in marriage for two agonizingly short years.

A knot formed in Teresa's stomach. "Mamá, I don't mean to be rude or ungrateful, but I don't want to go to Puerto Rico. Not now. Not ever."

Mamá put her hands on her ample hips and frowned. "Teresa, I'm worried about you. You used to be excited about life. Now all you do is go to work and to church. And when you're home, you spend most of your time in front of the TV, watching old romantic movies. My dear child, you can't go on like this."

Mamá was right. Teresa had put her life on pause. But how could she hit *play* again? Moving forward meant leaving behind the man who gave her life. The man who was her life.

"Mamá, I can't go to Puerto Rico. I just can't. Please understand."

"Teresa, I've tried to understand. But it's been five years since Roberto died. There comes a point when you have to let go of the past if you want to live in the present and have hope for the future. Isn't that what you tell your clients?"

8

Mamá's words stung. "There is no future for me without Roberto."

Mamá took her hands. "Teresa, listen to me. Roberto would hate to see you like this. Remember how much he loved life? He wants you to love life, too."

Teresa had never considered that Roberto might want her to move on with her life. "Okay, suppose I do go to Puerto Rico. What about living expenses while I'm there? A hotel in San Juan isn't cheap."

Mamá's eyes lit up. "That problem is solved, too. In her letter, Ramona invited you to stay at her beautiful inn free of charge. You will love it. It's right on the ocean." Mamá pressed her fingertips to her lips and kissed them in delight. "And she will also provide all of your meals."

Teresa raised an eyebrow. That left only her clients. And, truth be told, she didn't need to see them in her office. She could coach them by telephone or by Skype from anywhere in the world. That was one of the perks that had attracted her to the coaching profession in the first place, besides the opportunity to help transform people's lives.

And Ramona sounded desperate about her little granddaughter.

Mamá's eyes widened. "Well?"

"I'll think about it."

Mamá raised her hands in frustration. "*¡Teresita! Tu estás en la luna*! You have your head in the clouds. What's there to think about?"

"Mamá, you know I hate it when you're overbearing. I'm thirty-one years old. Just let me be while I think this through."

Mamá rubbed a hand across her forehead. "I'm sorry. I'm only trying to help."

Teresa pulled out a chair from the kitchen table. "I know. But the best help you can give me is to let me work things out on my own."

"You've been trying to work things out on your

own for five years now, and you're still depressed over Roberto."

Teresa's stomach boiled like a cauldron. "You seem to forget that he is my husband."

Mamá placed her hands on Teresa's shoulders. "He *was* your husband. He is now with the Lord and you are still here. You must go on with your life."

Teresa sank into a kitchen chair. Roberto's death had cut out her very heart, leaving her raw and broken. Unable to go on. Unable to dream.

To feel.

Her future had died with Roberto. She'd moved back in with her mother, hoping to assuage the grief. But now her pain had only grown worse. She could think of nothing else but her husband. The way he brought her coffee in the mornings. His beard tickling her face when he kissed her. His deep, bass voice when he read a passage of Scripture in their evening Bible studies. She would never forget him. How could she? She would never betray him by marrying another. Never leave him behind. Surely Mamá understood. She was a widow herself.

Yet, Mamá had managed to survive and even to love life again.

But how?

Teresa joined Mamá in saying grace. Then, taking a mouthful of *arroz con pollo*, she swallowed it together with the lump in her throat. Yes. She would go to Puerto Rico. Not for herself, but for Ramona's granddaughter.

Maybe she'd have more success helping Pilar than she'd had helping herself.

* * *

Teresa looked out the open back window of the taxi cab as it pulled up in front of *The Inn of the Dove* in Old San Juan. The charming, stuccoed structure stood on a tree-

10

lined street, just a stone's throw from the beach and filled with the fragrance of roses and bougainvillea. A black wrought-iron fence embraced the small front lawn that led to a spacious, wrap-around front porch.

Teresa paid the driver. "*Muchas gracias.*"

"*De nada, Señora.*"

She glanced at her wedding ring with pride. The driver had noticed and called her *Señora. Mrs.* An acknowledgment that she was married. Her trip was off to a good start.

She exited from the back seat while the driver removed her luggage from the trunk and set it just inside the fence. Then, after thanking her for her generous tip, he left.

Teresa stood for a moment admiring the charming inn she'd seen only in pictures. Its pale yellow façade, accented by royal blue shutters, was far more enchanting in person, a hidden oasis inviting one to rest and relax. But rest and relaxation would have to wait. She was here on business, not on vacation. Despite what Mamá thought.

Teresa picked up her luggage and started toward the porch but stopped short when she heard a man's voice behind her.

"Here. Let me help you."

At the sight of him, Teresa's insides warmed. Short in stature, but robust and tanned, he carried a pair of garden clippers in his right hand. His thick, dark hair framed a face that was not particularly handsome as much as it was kind. But what surprised her most were his blue eyes. Deep blue. So unusual for a Puerto Rican.

She straightened her shoulders. "Thank you. That's very kind of you." Why hadn't she refused his offer to carry her bags?

He smiled and covered the short distance between them in a single stride. As though reading her mind, he said, "At the *Inn of the Dove*, ladies never carry their luggage."

His words touched a vulnerable spot in her heart, a spot she'd missed in her relentless efforts to protect herself. She drew in a deep breath. His good manners reminded her of Roberto.

"By the way, my name is Marcos. Marcos Sanchez."

"Not Marcos Sanchez, Pilar's father?"

He nodded. "Precisely."

"I'm sorry I didn't recognize you. I thought you were the gardener."

He laughed. "I'm that, too. In fact, I was mowing the lawn when you arrived." His laughter was like a waterfall cascading over a cliff. Strong and powerful. "And you must be Doctor Teresa Lopez Gonzalez, the life coach I hired and the famous daughter of Marisol Lopez. My mother has often spoken of your mother and of their childhood friendship."

Bracing herself against the slight tug of her heart, Teresa extended her hand in greeting. "*Mucho gusto.*"

He rested one suitcase on the ground.

As he shook her hand, the warmth of his hand against hers troubled the stagnant waters of her grieving heart, pushing them to the edge of life. She quickly pushed them back.

"*Encantado.* Delighted to meet you."

She tensed. Five years of grief were taking their toll on her. Making her vulnerable to emotions long buried. She must not forget she was here on business.

And business only.

Chapter Two

Teresa followed Marcos into the spacious lobby. Her gaze scanned her new surroundings. The inn was lovely. Four exquisite Queen Anne chairs upholstered with a vibrant floral design surrounded a round mahogany table on which sat a magnificent bouquet of white orchids. In one corner, a fountain gurgled while its clear water streamed into a wide, lotus-shaped basin.

She drank in the elegant atmosphere as she approached the reception desk. Behind it stood a well-coiffed, well-manicured middle-aged woman in a bright yellow sundress. She looked up and smiled. "Welcome to the *Inn of the Dove*.

Marcos set Teresa's luggage on the floor. "Mamá, this is Teresa, Marisol's daughter."

The woman's eyes widened with delight, and she gave a shout and a single loud clap. "Oh, *gracias a Dios*!" She rushed from behind the counter and embraced Teresa. "Teresita. Precious daughter of my friend. The last time I saw you, you were four years old. Now you are a beautiful, grown woman. Welcome back to Puerto Rico." She hugged her tightly.

Teresa's cheeks grew warm. "Thank you, *Señora* Sanchez."

"Forget the *Señora* Sanchez. Just call me Ramona."

"*Gracias*, Ramona. My mother sends you her love."

"Ah, how is my dear friend Marisol? We have been friends since we were this high." She measured a young child's height with her palm. "I have some good stories to tell you about your Mamá. But they can wait for later. Now, we will show you to your room so you can relax and freshen up. We will be serving dinner at six o'clock, but refreshments are always available on the back veranda."

Ramona turned to Marcos. "Marcos, please take Teresa's luggage to her room."

"Si, Mamá. I would be honored."

Teresa caught Marcos' penetrating gaze. A gaze that spoke of suffering.

A gaze that understood pain.

A pang of guilt struck Teresa's heart. Why was she even going there? What difference did it make to her if Marcos had suffered? Besides, she was here to help Pilar, not Marcos.

And most of all, she was a married woman. And faithful married women did not allow themselves to become embroiled with the problems of other men.

Straightening her shoulders, she followed Marcos down a long, winding corridor to a room in the eastern wing of the inn. As she walked, she studied the man leading the way before her. His broad shoulders, taut with the weight of the luggage, reminded her of one who had learned early on to carry the burdens of life.

A rush of compassion filled her soul. How difficult it must be to raise a child alone! She would do her best to help Pilar.

When they reached the door of the suite, Marcos inserted the key then opened the door without entering. "Ladies first." He smiled.

Teresa entered a lovely suite, large and spacious, with a king-size bed and a cozy sitting room beyond the sleeping area. A small deck overlooked a lovely garden burgeoning with crimson and yellow hibiscus. In the distance, the Atlantic Ocean shimmered in the early afternoon sunlight.

Marcos brought in her bags. "The view from this room at sunrise is amazing."

Teresa walked to the open window and looked out.

Even now, in late afternoon, the view took her breath away. Ribbons of sunlight shimmering over emerald green water. Cool breezes wafting in from ocean surf. Foamy waves lapping against sandy shores, soothing her heart.

She folded her arms across her chest. "I remember, as a child, walking with my mother on the beach in the early hours of the morning when we lived here. I used to run ahead of her to search for seashells." She turned toward Marcos. "I even started a collection I still have. Mamá keeps it in a cabinet in our dining room." She smiled. "Every now and then I take it out and feel the beautiful texture of the shells and put them against my ear to listen to the sounds of the ocean."

"You have a good memory."

She pondered his words for a moment. "Yes, I do. Perhaps too good."

His face grew solemn. "I understand."

Something inside her connected with him. Against her will.

Marcos cleared his throat. "Well, please make yourself at home. Later, when you're ready, we can discuss my daughter Pilar's situation." He lowered his eyes then looked up. "I'm so grateful for your willingness to come all the way to Puerto Rico to help her."

His words touched her heart. "It's my pleasure."

He bowed slightly. "Now I'll leave you to your own thoughts." He shut the door behind him.

Her own thoughts. What were her own thoughts? She didn't know anymore. Her mind and heart were a mumble-jumble of conflicting thoughts and emotions. Perhaps it was the new environment or the tropical air of Puerto Rico. For whatever reason, she felt more emotionally vulnerable in this place. More subject to her feelings.

More prone to question her resolve regarding Roberto.

She sank into the soft king-size bed and vehemently shook her head. No. She would not allow her resolve to weaken. She would not betray Roberto's memory, no matter how many conflicting thoughts and feelings she experienced.

No matter how lonely her heart.

No matter how kind and attentive Marcos Sanchez might be.

* * *

Marcos headed back to the lobby to check for recent guest arrivals. His first meeting with Marisol's daughter had been more pleasant than he'd expected. For one thing, Teresa had shattered his preconceived notion of what a life coach looked like. For some crazy reason, he'd expected a sturdy woman in conservative black pumps wearing her hair short and closely cropped. Instead, he'd discovered an elegant woman stylishly coiffed and impeccably dressed who carried herself with the poise of a queen. Most important, she had a tender heart. Why else would she come all the way to Puerto Rico to help Pilar?

Rounding the corner of the hallway, he strode into the lobby and stopped at the reception desk. His mother stood behind it, her eyes on the computer screen.

She looked up at him and gave him a knowing smile. "So. What do you think of Teresa?"

Marcos' face flushed. Mamá was the Puerto Rican version of a Jewish Yenta. For years, she'd been pressing him to find a wife who would be a good helpmate for him and a fitting mother for Pilar.

Ramona placed her hands on her hips and chuckled. "Have you nothing to say, my dear, thick-headed son?"

His stomach tensed. "What do you want me to say, Mamá? She's here to help Pilar. Nothing more."

Ramona exhaled a long breath of air. "Nothing more unless you make it something more."

16

Marcos tensed. "Mamá, how many times do I have to tell you I'm a grown man and can make my own decisions?" Although he was thirty-four years old, Mamá still treated him like a little boy. "Besides, Teresa is here on business, and I will respect that fact. It would be totally inappropriate for me to do otherwise."

Ramona gave him a gentle poke in the chest. "Tell me you didn't find her attractive. I dare you." Totally ignoring his objections, she wagged a finger in his face.

He'd never lied to Mamá, and he wouldn't start now. "Yes, I did find her attractive." He could not restrain a smile. "Very attractive."

A smug look appeared on Mamá's face. "There. See. I knew it. I know my Marcos."

He couldn't deny Mamá read him like a book. "Okay, Mamá. So you knew it. Now what of it? I don't even know Teresa. Just because a woman is attractive on the outside doesn't mean she's attractive on the inside."

"That's true." Mamá laughed.

Well, at least Mamá was humble enough to concede he was right on that point.

"But she is Marisol's daughter. That should tell you something."

He furrowed an eyebrow. "What should it tell me?"

"That she was raised according to the Word of God."

"Being raised according to the Word of God and living according to the Word of God are two different things."

"Yes, but Teresa is a devout follower of Christ. Marisol told me."

An image of two scheming mothers flashed across Marcos' mind. "What have you and Marisol been up to? Have you been scheming behind the backs of your children?"

A mischievous look crossed Mamá's face. "The schemes of two old friends regarding their children are none of your business." She averted his gaze.

"Ha! So, you admit you're guilty." He gave her an affectionate peck on the cheek.

Ramona laughed. "Guilty as charged. And not one bit remorseful about it." She grew serious. "Marcos, listen to me." She laid a hand on her son's shoulder and looked up at him. "I want only your happiness. It isn't every day a good woman presents herself, a woman who just happens to be the daughter of my best friend." Ramona tilted her head. "Could it be the Lord is answering my prayer?"

His neck tensed. "*Your* prayer maybe, Mamá, but not mine."

"Marcos, I know you've been praying for a good wife and for a mother for Pilar."

How did Mamá know? He'd never told her.

She placed both hands on his shoulders. "I ask only one thing of you. Listen to the voice of the Holy Spirit. Then do what He says."

He stifled his annoyance. "I'm sorry, Mamá. I know you mean well."

She playfully slapped him upside the head. "I always mean well when it comes to my only son." She tugged on his ear. "Listen to Holy Spirit. And then obey what He tells you to do."

No use trying to win an argument with Mamá. He smiled and changed the subject. "Now, will you please tell me if we have any more guest arrivals who need help with their luggage?"

She beamed a victorious smile. "None at the moment, but I'll page you when we do."

* * *

Teresa unpacked her suitcases and put her clothes in

the closet and dresser drawers. This would be her home for the next three months while she coached Pilar, so she might as well settle in and get comfortable.

The lovely suite lacked no amenity. A small refrigerator stood in the corner. She opened it and, to her pleasant surprise, found it stocked with fresh bottled juices and several bottles of spring water. A small microwave oven sat atop the refrigerator, and next to it, a basket overflowed with microwavable muffins and pastries of all sorts. A compact stovetop completed the kitchenette area, providing all she needed for her culinary comfort. Of course, at Ramona's kind invitation, Teresa would take her main meals in the dining room, but for those moments when she wanted a quick, do-it-yourself repast, she had everything she needed. To top it all off, a crystal vase of freshly-cut yellow roses graced the small round table in front of the loveseat. Ramona had thought of everything. Teresa couldn't have asked for anything more.

She opened the broad French doors and stepped out onto the deck. Two white Adirondack chairs covered with bright yellow and red-striped cushions sat in front of a glass-topped round table with its own vase of fresh yellow roses. A hummingbird chirped happily as it hovered over a white orchid, drinking in its sweet nectar. In the distance, the emerald green Atlantic Ocean sparkled like millions of diamonds under the brilliant tropical sun.

Teresa drew in a deep breath of the fresh ocean air. Amazing how a change of environment could affect one's mood—and one's perspective. The taut nerves she'd had in New Jersey had relaxed now that she was in San Juan. Who said that climate didn't affect one's attitude?

Her thoughts drifted to Marcos. She hadn't expected to find him so charming. So attentive.

So kind.

Mamá had rarely spoken of Ramona's son, except to say that he was having a hard time with his daughter Pilar.

That raising a troubled teenager all alone was no picnic. But, apart from feeling a twinge of compassion for Ramona's son, Teresa had dismissed Mamá's comments with little more than a quick prayer for the widower's plight. Her own sorrow over losing Roberto had overshadowed everyone else's.

But now that she'd met Marcos in person, his plight had taken on a more personal dimension. Indeed, the whole reason she was here was because of Marcos' plight. Meeting the man behind the name had changed the game. Maybe Mamá was right. She was here to help him as well as his daughter. She'd use her coaching skills to the best of her ability to help Pilar find her way. In the process, she'd help a hurting man who just happened to be the son of her mother's best friend. Having done both, she'd return to New Jersey with a sense of accomplishment at having brought some good to their world.

Teresa went back inside. Her plans to take a nap evaporated in the sultriness of the tropical afternoon. There'd be time to sleep that night. Now, she'd freshen up and take advantage of those refreshments Ramona had said would be available on the back veranda.

After a quick shower, Teresa donned a pair of white slacks and a red sleeveless blouse. Red was her best color. At least, that's what everyone told her. Standing before the bathroom mirror, she ran a brush through her long, black wavy hair and slid a tube of crimson lipstick across her lips. She patted them with a tissue and then applied a touch of black mascara to her hazel eyes. For the first time in a long time, life stirred within her. Yes, ever so slightly, but it stirred, nonetheless. She shrugged her shoulders. Must be the Puerto Rican air. It was filled with fragrances that aroused and stimulated the senses in a way that New Jersey air did not.

If only Roberto could be here to share the beauty with her.

Chapter Three

Marcos wielded the heavy pruning shears with the deftness of a professional gardener. Ever since his parents had purchased the old inn twenty years earlier, when he was just fourteen years old, he'd worked at keeping the grounds looking good. When his father died a year later, Marcos was put in charge of all the landscaping. At first, he'd complained that he'd rather be playing soccer. But it didn't take long for him to realize how much he loved landscaping and what a talent he had for it. Ever since then, he'd won many awards for his splendid gardens and had turned the *Inn of the Dove* into one of the most beautiful places to stay while in old San Juan.

As he clipped the lavender bougainvillea, his thoughts locked onto Teresa. She was more beautiful than he'd expected. Not that beauty was everything. But her beauty went beyond the surface. There was an inner beauty about her that touched his heart in a way that no other woman had touched it since the death of his precious wife Marguerita. Thirteen years of living without her had taken their toll on him. And, with a severely depressed teenage daughter on his hands, sometimes life seemed more than he could handle. Teresa's arrival had brought him hope regarding Pilar. Now, if only Pilar were as excited as he was about what Teresa could do for her.

His thoughts shifted to his only child. When he'd first told her about Teresa, Pilar had balked.

"I refuse to talk to a total stranger."

"But she's not a total stranger. She's the daughter of your grandmother's best friend."

Pilar crossed her arms across her chest. "She's a

total stranger to me."

No amount of explaining could convince the child. Only after Marcos had pled with her to give coaching a try had Pilar relented.

She wasn't a rebellious or defiant child. Sometimes he wished she *were* rebellious instead of depressed all the time. At least he'd know there was still life left within her.

Still hope.

But her growing depression worried him. Sometimes she'd go for days on end hardly talking to anyone and, worse yet, hardly eating a thing. Made him wish all over again that Marguerita had not died in childbirth. A girl Pilar's age needed the nurturing only a mother could give.

And he needed the support only a wife could provide.

Marcos stopped to wipe his brow. The all-too familiar sense of helplessness seeped into his soul. "Lord, help me help Pilar. Show me what to do and what not to do. What to say and what not to say. Help me to be the father she needs at this difficult time in her life."

"The gardens here are absolutely lovely."

Teresa's voice jolted him from his prayerful reverie. He looked up. The image of her he'd held in his mind only a few short moments ago suddenly took human form before his eyes. Except the human form far surpassed in beauty the mental image. His heart stirred. *"Buenas tardes.* I didn't see you standing there." He lowered the shears to his side.

"That's because I just stepped out here. I went to the back veranda but no one was around." She smiled. "I hope I'm not interrupting."

"No, of course not." Had she heard him praying for Pilar?

He laid the shears behind a bush and walked toward the front steps. The way the sun danced over her dark tresses made him wonder how it would feel to caress them.

"I could use a cool drink myself. Mind if I join you?"

She smiled. "Not at all. I'd enjoy the company. Besides, I think we need to talk about Pilar before I start her coaching sessions."

He nodded. "Yes, I agree."

Two by two, he climbed the steps to the porch. "Let me go wash up first. I'll meet you in the lobby in about ten minutes, and then we'll walk back to the veranda together."

"That's fine."

Taking his leave, Marcos jogged down the long hall to his private quarters, reminding himself that, no matter what Mamá said, Teresa was here on business.

Strictly business.

* * *

As she waited for Marcos, Teresa wandered around the charming lobby, admiring its stylish décor and beautiful floral displays. Ramona certainly knew how to arrange flowers. And Marcos certainly knew how to grow them. Clusters of purple hydrangeas, pink roses, and yellow daffodils brightened a room that was already bright with the afternoon sun. Their fragrance filled the air with an exotic perfume unlike anything she'd ever experienced in New Jersey, a place and a life that, moment by moment, were fading into a distant past.

A few house guests sat in the lobby, chatting quietly. In the corner, an elderly gentleman dozed while holding a folded newspaper on his lap.

Teresa's gaze scanned the lobby. A framed photograph on a corner table caught her eye. She picked up the photograph to study it more closely. A smileless man stood with his back to the ocean, holding a small child by the hand. The child too was without a smile. Teresa studied the photo. She recognized a much younger Marcos. The little child was very likely his daughter. Teresa had not yet met Pilar, but the resemblance of the child in the photo to Marcos was unmistakable. She studied the photo, looking for emotional clues in their sorrowful faces. Clues that would help her decipher the enigma of Pilar's depression.

"That photo was taken eleven years ago, when Pilar was only two."

At the sound of Marcos' voice, Teresa swung around, nearly dropping the photograph. "Why, hello. I didn't see you there." Her heart pounded against her will.

He smiled. "Now we're even. I didn't see you earlier on the porch, either."

There was something in the way he looked at her that unsettled her and put her emotions on high alert. It was the same way Roberto had looked at her shortly after she'd met him nearly eight years before.

She straightened her shoulders and stiffened her heart. "You took me by surprise."

He moved closer. "You took me by surprise, too."

She took a step backward. "When?"

"When you first arrived. I was expecting someone, well, a little more staid and professional."

She suppressed a smile. "Are you saying I don't look professional?" She leaned over to replace the photograph on the table.

"Not exactly. I guess a better word would be *clinical*." He accented the comment with a gesture of his hand. "You don't look clinical."

His obvious discomfort touched her. "I find that if I present a more casual demeanor, my clients tend to open up to me better. Sometimes, however, there's a fine line between professional and friendly. I have to be aware of that line at all times." She spoke the words more for herself than for him.

He shoved both hands into his pockets. "I hope I didn't insult you. I didn't mean to. It's just that—well, I didn't expect you to be so beautiful."

Heat flooded Teresa's cheeks like lava erupting from a volcano. Why did he have to say that? Didn't he know she was here only on business? That she was off limits?

And off limits forever?

He gently took her by the elbow. "Let's go to the veranda. There's always a cool breeze there."

A long hallway led from the lobby to the veranda. Beautiful watercolor paintings of San Juan hung along the walls on each side, creating a lovely entrance into an even lovelier veranda. To Teresa's great dismay, walking by the side of Ramona's son felt so right. So comfortable. Like wearing an old pair of cozy slippers or drinking hot chocolate by the fireplace on a cold winter night.

She drew in a deep breath and lassoed her thoughts.

Marcos was right. The breeze on the veranda was cool and refreshing. Blowing in from the Atlantic, it carried the clean smell of salt mingled with the aroma of the flowers it brushed on its way.

Marcos pulled out a chair for her. "Please. Sit down. I'll get us something cold to drink." He walked over to a large refrigerator with a clear glass door. It was stocked with all kinds of delicious beverages for the convenience of house guests. "Let's see. We have *limonata*, orange juice, and iced tea. Which would you prefer?"

"Lemonade sounds great." She settled into the large wicker chair and watched Marcos pour the drinks. His calloused hands were those of a man accustomed to heavy work outdoors.

Marcos handed her the glass of lemonade, his hand slightly brushing hers. A chill skittered across Teresa's skin. Guilt washed over her.

He took a seat on the chair across from her. "Well, how do you like Puerto Rico so far?"

Her thoughts hung between Hoboken and San Juan. "I'm still processing everything. In a strange way, I feel as though I've come back to my roots."

He laughed a laugh that warmed her to the core. "Perhaps you feel that way because you *have* come back to your roots."

Her muscles tensed. The conversation was heading in a direction she didn't want to go. "So, tell me about Pilar."

His face grew serious as he shook his head. "Ah, Pilar. My precious Pilar. What is there to say except I don't recognize her anymore?" He let out a long breath. "She's not the daughter I once knew. She has become a virtual stranger to me and to her *abuela*. Needless to say, we are quite concerned about her."

Teresa settled back in her chair and switched to life coach mode. A comfortable mode. A mode that put her on her own turf. "And who was that daughter you once knew?"

His gaze looked right through her, as though seeing something beyond her he wished to recall. "That's a very good question. Pilar has always been a quiet child. Introverted even, with a tendency to keep to herself. When she was a little girl, her grandmother and I had to encourage her to play with her little cousins and her classmates at school. Even then, she remained apart as much as she could, unwilling to engage in the activities of the other children." He looked down. "She seemed happiest when she was alone."

Teresa nodded. A case of unprocessed grief, with all of its attendant manifestations.

She studied him, his face revealing the deep aching in his paternal heart. Compassion gripped her.

Marcos lifted his gaze toward her. "But lately, she not only wants to keep to herself. She seems deeply depressed and has lost her appetite." He put down his glass on the table beside him and straightened. "Truth be told, I'm worried sick about her. I've tried everything I know how to do. I've taken her to see a counselor. I've encouraged her to go out with her friends. I've even encouraged her to pursue tennis, a sport she loves. But nothing has worked. She has even lost interest in her youth group at church, a group that used to mean everything to her. The distance between us is widening. I'd reached the end of my rope when my mother suggested I get help. She told me Marisol's daughter was a life coach." He smiled. "That's when I decided to hire you." He leaned forward, his eyes deep with pain, and folded his hands. "I hope you'll be able to help my little girl."

Teresa heard the desperation in his voice. "I will do my best, Mr. Sanchez. I promise you."

"Marcos. Please call me Marcos."

She nodded but would not concede the same familiarity on his part toward her. It would be too dangerous.

The screen door creaked open and Pilar entered the veranda, her long brown hair covering half her face. Her head hung low and her shoulders slumped.

"*Hola*, Pilar." Marcos rose and gave his daughter a hug she resisted. His arm still around her shoulder, he drew her toward Teresa. "I'd like you to meet Doctor Teresa Gonzalez, your new life coach."

The child held back, her gaze fixed on the floor.

Teresa rose and extended a hand in greeting. "*Hola*, Pilar. I'm very happy to meet you."

Still no response.

Marcos prodded. "Pilar, please acknowledge Doctor Gonzalez."

Teresa laid a hand on Marcos' arm. "It's all right. We'll get to know each other in due time." Then, turning toward the young girl, she offered her best unreciprocated smile.

* * *

"Pilar, you embarrassed me in front of Doctor Gonzalez." Marcos paced the living room of the private apartment he and his daughter shared in the western wing of the *Inn of the Dove*. He didn't want to fuss at her, but she'd been rude toward Teresa, and he would not permit rudeness toward anyone. "She came all the way from New Jersey to help you. You could at least have acknowledged her with a nod or a hand shake." He raked his fingers through his hair. "What am I going to do with you?"

Pilar sat looking dejected on the sofa, one leg tucked under her, her hands folded in her lap.

His chest ached. With her lovely, dark, almond-shaped eyes, she looked more and more like her mother every day. His precious Marguerita.

A lump formed in his throat.

"I'm sorry, Papa. I just didn't know what to say. I wasn't trying to be rude. It's just that it's hard for me to meet new people."

Marcos swallowed his exasperation and sat by his daughter. "Honey, I'm quite concerned about you. You've changed. You're not the Pilar I once knew."

Her face contorted as she balled her fists. She jumped up from the couch and turned toward him, her cheeks aflame, her arms straight at her side. "Did you ever really *know* me, Papa?" Her voice railed like a lashing whip. "Did you? Did you ever really care about how I feel?" Darts of accusation shot from her fiery black eyes.

Why was she so angry with him?

She threw her hands in the air. "No! You've never really cared about how I feel. All you've ever cared about is this stupid inn. How you have to make it a success." She spat out the words like dirt. "Well, I don't care one bit about the *Inn of the Dove*. As far as I'm concerned, it could be the *Inn of the Crow*. I don't care if it succeeds or fails. All this place has ever done for me is stolen my papa." Her voice caught and her body trembled. "Wasn't it bad enough that death stole my mother? Did I have to lose my father, too?" She broke into sobs and ran toward the door.

Marcos' heart reeled. Should he cringe in anguish at her words or be thankful she'd shown some life, even if she'd expressed that life through rage?

He caught her and drew her close, cradling her head in his shoulder as sobs wracked her frail, young body. A sharp ache rose from the deepest part of his being and lodged in his throat. If only he'd known the depth of his daughter's pain. If only he'd been more sensitive.

If only Marguerita had not died.

Hot tears stung his eyes and streamed down his face. He stroked his daughter's hair and swallowed hard. All these years he'd been so absorbed with his own pain at losing his wife that he hadn't considered the pain of their only child.

Remorse flooded his soul. "O God, forgive me."

For several guilt-ridden moments, he held his daughter tightly in his arms.

Finally, her trembling subsided and her body relaxed. "I want to go to my room."

Marcos grabbed her hand as she pulled away. "Can we talk first?"

"It's too late to talk, Papa. I have nothing to say to you. I just don't care anymore."

Icy talons clawed at Marcos' soul. "Would you be willing to talk with Doctor Gonzalez?"

Pilar shuffled a foot. "What good would that do?"

Marcos released his daughter's hand. "Maybe, because she's a woman, she will understand you better than I do."

Pilar's eyes narrowed. "There was only one woman who could understand me." His child's lips quivered. "And she's dead!"

A sword pierced Marcos' heart as his daughter fled, sobbing, from the room.

Chapter Four

Teresa sat by the open window of her sitting room. A gentle breeze blew through the wooden slats, bringing with it the fresh salt air of the Atlantic Ocean. A full moon hung low over the garden, spreading milky white ribbons of light over the manicured lawn. Blossom-laden branches of a Flamboyant tree cast soft shadows in the moonlight. From the nearby veranda, the cheerful voices of chattering guests filled the evening atmosphere with life and laughter.

She sighed. The nearly four-hour flight from New Jersey and the flurry of activities during the day had caught up with her. She'd sleep well tonight.

Or so she hoped.

She stretched her legs and sighed. Pilar's reaction to meeting her had not in the least offended her. On the contrary, to Teresa's professional eye, it indicated the depth of pain Pilar carried within her. The poor child. To have to go through life without a mother had to be one of the hardest things in the world. Even a warm and loving grandmother like Ramona couldn't take the place of one's own mother.

Thank You, Lord, for my mother. Mamá could surely be overbearing, but what a blessing she was. After Roberto's untimely death, it was Mamá who had stood by her, comforting her and sustaining her. Taking care of all the daily details Teresa had been too emotionally paralyzed to take care of. Giving her a shoulder to sob on.

What would she have done without Mamá?

Teresa glanced at her wristwatch. Too late to call her tonight. Teresa would call her in the morning, just to tell her how much she loved her.

With a touch of homesickness, Teresa rose from her seat at the window and shed the light cotton shrug she'd donned for dinner. She threw it on the bed. Stretching her arms above her head, she scanned the lovely suite before her. Ramona had thought of everything, down to the lotus-shaped crystal plate filled with Godiva chocolates on the night stand. Not only were the surroundings lovely, but the atmosphere exuded serenity and peace. Staying at the *Inn of the Dove* was like staying in a royal palace. Mamá was right. Ramona was the consummate hostess, offering her guests the best in cuisine, accommodations, and service. The love of Christ shone brightly through this precious woman.

The woman who had birthed Marcos Sanchez.

A rush of forgotten longings flooded Teresa's soul. Longings for Roberto's arms enfolding her in his embrace. The feel of his hand caressing her cheek.

The warm touch of his lips on hers.

She squeezed her eyes shut and forced herself to squelch the emotions that tugged at her heart. Being away from home made one vulnerable to feelings easily suppressed in her normal environment. She hadn't realized how much she missed Roberto.

How much she missed the love of a man.

She gathered her toiletries and her night gown and proceeded to the bathroom. Maybe a warm bath and a good night's rest would put her senses back on track.

At least, she hoped so.

* * *

Marcos glanced at the grandfather clock in his living room. Seven past midnight. He'd been sitting there for three hours, grieving and praying.

Worrying about Pilar.

32

Her emotional exit from the room had left a hole in his heart. A hole from which he could not climb out.

He rubbed his forehead. "Father God, forgive me for worrying. I am at my wits' end with Pilar. My heart is broken because her heart is broken."

My son, I understand your pain. My heart breaks when your heart breaks.

A lump formed in Marcos' throat. God was there for him. God would help him.

God knew his name.

"Thank you, Father." The words came from the depths of his heart.

The depths of his pain.

He rested his elbows on his knees. This single parenting thing was becoming more and more of a challenge as Pilar grew older. If Pilar had been a son, things might have been easier. But the volatile emotions of a teenage daughter, coupled with the trauma of the tragic loss of her mother, made dealing with Pilar overwhelming.

He drew in a deep breath. How much longer could he be both father and mother to his little girl? How much longer could he worry and fret over what to do about her?

He swallowed hard. How much longer could he face life's challenges alone?

He needed help.

You need Teresa.

Marcos started. Where did that come from?

He sat up straight, his heart trembling. "Lord, was that You?"

But only silence came in reply.

* * *

Teresa awakened the next morning to the sound of starlings trilling outside her window. Although it was only six o'clock, the sun had already made major headway in its journey across the sky. Its rays filtered through the closed window blinds, casting a soft yellow glow across the room.

She stretched and lingered a few moments longer in the comfortable king-size bed. The aroma of freshly brewed coffee wafted into her room from the nearby veranda. She took a deep breath, hoping the prospect of hot coffee would prompt her to get out of bed.

She fluffed her pillow for another five minutes of rest. This morning she would meet with Pilar for their first coaching session. Marcos had made arrangements for them to use a small private office on the second floor, away from the hustle-bustle of the lobby. There she could work with Pilar in the privacy required for the coach-client relationship.

At the ring of the telephone, she remembered she'd requested a wake-up call. She reached toward the telephone on the night stand and lifted the receiver. "Good morning."

A recorded voice greeted her. "Good morning. This is your wake-up call. Have a good day." Good thing Spanish was her mother tongue. When Mamá had arrived in New Jersey, she didn't know a word of English. So she spoke to Teresa in Spanish. Being bi-lingual was definitely an asset in this day and age.

Teresa almost replied to the telephone message but then remembered she was talking to a computerized voice. Releasing a giggle, she replaced the receiver and rose from the bed. Taking her robe from the back of the chair where she'd laid it the night before, she wrapped the garment around her and headed toward the window. She opened the blinds just a crack and peered through the slats.

Her heart leapt at the sight of Marcos trimming a rose bush in front of the veranda. Hoping he hadn't seen her, she quickly closed the blinds and made her way to the bathroom.

What is wrong with me? I'm acting like a silly school girl.

After dressing, she called Mamá on her cell phone.

"Teresita! I am so happy to hear from you."

Hearing Mamá's voice helped her to re-establish her bearings. "*Hola*, Mamá. I just wanted to call to tell you I love you."

"I love you, too, Teresita, and I miss you. Oh, how I miss you!"

Teresa smiled as tears filled her eyes. "I miss you, too, Mamá."

"So, tell me. How was your flight? How are things going in beautiful Puerto Rico? How is Ramona? And Marcos? Have you met Marcos? And Pilar?"

Teresa chuckled. Mamá's excitement was contagious. "I'll answer your questions one at a time. First, my flight was good. Second, I met Ramona and love her. Now I know the reason she is your best friend. Third, I met Marcos and his daughter Pilar. They are both very nice, although Pilar seemed a bit shy. We begin coaching sessions this morning. Fourth, Puerto Rico is breathtakingly beautiful. I wish you could have come with me."

"I do, too. Lord willing, I will get to see my native land once again. Are you eating well?"

Teresa laughed. Mamá would forever look on her as her little girl. "Yes, Mamá. I'm eating very well. The food here is delicious."

"And the weather?"

"The weather is beautiful. Warm, balmy. The temperature is perfect."

"I'm so glad you're there, Teresita. Already I can sense the trip has done wonders for your soul."

"I'm feeling more relaxed. That's for sure. It's hard not to in this tropical paradise."

There was a slight pause on Mamá's end. "So, what do you think of Marcos?"

There it was. The bomb Teresa had been dreading. "Mamá, have you been scheming with Ramona?"

"Me? Scheming?" Another pause, followed by laughter. "Yes."

Teresa laughed, too, in spite of herself. Mamá could not tell a lie if her life depended on it. "I think Marcos is a very nice man—and a hurting father."

"Maybe the Lord sent you there to help him as well as Pilar."

Teresa stiffened. "Well, in helping Pilar I will certainly be helping her father. Each affects the other."

"That's true."

Teresa changed the subject. "How are you, Mamá?"

"I'm fine. Bearing the cold weather as best I can. I've been cooking some meals and freezing them for your return."

"Thank you. You are good to me."

"I love you, Teresita, and am praying for you. Enjoy yourself. And stay in touch."

"I will, Mamá. I love you, too."

Teresa pressed the button on her cell phone to end the call. Hearing Mamá's voice was just what she needed before facing the day.

A day that might prove to be quite a difficult one.

* * *

A few moments later, Teresa was on her way to breakfast on the veranda. Why did she hope she'd find Marcos still trimming the rosebush?

She resisted the sinful thought and prayed for forgiveness.

She found a seat closest to the ocean. The sight of the white, foaming waves of the Atlantic against the emerald blue of its depths soothed her troubled soul.

Forget those things that are behind.

The Lord's words caught her by surprise. They were the same words Mamá had been speaking to her ever since Roberto's death.

"But, Lord, how can I forget Roberto? He was my life!"

I'm not asking you to forget Roberto, dear one. He will always be a part of your heart. I'm asking you to live in the now. That is where you will find life. In the now. That is where I am. In the now.

A waiter came to take her order, interrupting her thoughts and bringing with him a pot of much-needed black coffee.

"*Buenos días, Señora.* Would you like some coffee?"

"Yes, please."

As Teresa watched, the waiter filled the lovely China cup. Ramona's good taste prevailed even to the dishes used in the veranda café.

Teresa sipped the strong black coffee as she waited for her breakfast to arrive. It tasted so good she didn't need to add her usual teaspoonful of sugar.

Subdued chatter filled the area as couples, young and old, sat at cozy, round tables enjoying their breakfasts and one another. Teresa's heart clenched. Roberto would have loved this place. So often, they'd spoken of taking a vacation in their parents' homeland, but something always came up to prevent them from doing so. Tomorrow always seemed a certainty, especially when one was young and in love.

But tomorrow never came, and now it was too late.

A pang of remorse struck her heart. She blinked back the tears that sprang to her eyes. She would not allow herself to wallow in sorrow. No. Not now. Not when she had to be strong in order to encourage Pilar. How could she show Pilar she had a future when she didn't see one for herself?

Teresa took a deep breath. She must remember she was here on business, and business demanded putting aside one's personal problems and focusing on the client.

She looked beyond the railing to the garden. Any hope of seeing Marcos had vanished when she'd stepped foot on the veranda. He was nowhere in sight. He must have finished his gardening and moved on to something else. Just as well. She could not allow anything—or anyone—to distract her from her mission to help Pilar.

And to be faithful to Roberto's memory.

"Your eggs, madam." The waiter appeared at her side.

"Thank you." She lowered her head and prayed a blessing over her food.

The croissant was fresh and warm. Taking a dollop of jam from the small container, she spread it generously over the bread and took a bite. The pastry's delicate texture melted in her mouth, caressing her palate with the rich taste of butter and cream.

"May I join you?"

She started, nearly choking on the morsel in her mouth. Hastening to finish chewing the piece of croissant and to swallow it, she kept her head down for a moment. When she looked up, Marcos was standing by her chair, a nervous look on his face while waiting for her reply.

Teresa tapped a napkin against her lips. "Uh . . . of course you may join me." She gathered her wits about her and smiled. "You *are*, after all, the father of my young client who is a minor." Always remember to keep things professional.

Marcos pulled out the chair next to hers and sat down.

She breathed in the musky scent of his cologne, her senses stirring and her brain rocketing to high alert.

He shifted in his seat. "So, today is the big day." The twitching in his nose betrayed him.

"You seem nervous."

He smiled. "You noticed."

She smiled back. "I'm trained to notice."

"I could take that as an encouraging statement or a scary one."

Teresa laughed. "How about taking it as an encouraging one? I'm trained to help, not to frighten."

"Whew! For a minute there, I thought you were seeing right through me. I felt like a goldfish in a fishbowl." He wiped the back of his hand across his brow in a pretense of discomfort. "Not a good feeling, I might add."

Before realizing what she was doing, she placed a comforting hand on his then quickly withdrew it, but not before wishing she could keep it there. "So, tell me. Why are you nervous?"

"I'm not sure. I was up half the night worrying about . . ." He fumbled for the right words.

"About whether or not this coaching thing is going to work?"

He looked at her for a long moment. "Yes. That's precisely what I was worrying about. How did you know?"

"Let's say I've been down that road before with other clients."

He nodded. "Okay. I'm afraid this coaching thing isn't going to work. Everything else I've tried to help Pilar has failed—even counseling—so what makes me think coaching is going to work?"

She straightened into full coaching mode. "What makes you think it won't?"

He scratched his head. "Well, you ask a good question. Maybe I don't have the faith to believe." He chuckled. "Maybe I'm the one who's depressed." He lowered his voice. "I guess your past doesn't have to equal your future, does it?"

Like a flash of lightning illuminating a blackened sky, his words jolted her into a new reality. *Your past doesn't have to equal your future.* Could it be she'd been expecting her past with Roberto to equal her future? That she'd been expecting to live that past as her future? That she'd closed herself off to any future at all by living in the past? Did not Scripture command one to forget those things that lie behind and to reach forth to those things that lie ahead?

She lowered her voice to almost a whisper. "No, Marcos. Your past does not have to equal your future." She spoke the words more for herself than for him.

But saying the words was one thing. Living them out was quite another.

Chapter Five

Teresa sat at the elegant mahogany desk, waiting for Pilar. The early afternoon sun filtered through the half-open vertical blinds, casting a soft glow to the charming office Marcos had provided for her coaching sessions. The small but comfortable room was perfect, with its leather sofa, two upholstered chairs, and a mahogany coffee table that matched the desk. A Victorian floor lamp just behind the sofa added an extra warm touch to an already warm room. Situated on the second floor on the inn's eastern side, the office was far enough away from the inn's activities to afford the privacy and quiet she needed.

Teresa clicked the ballpoint pen in her hand. Despite intense training and extensive experience, her nerves jangled at the prospect of working with Pilar. Maybe it was the fact she was Ramona's granddaughter. Almost like family. And working with family could end up in disaster.

She tapped her pen several times on the blank page of the yellow legal pad before her. Pilar was ten minutes late for her first appointment. Not unusual for someone who didn't want to be coached in the first place. But still a sign of potential trouble.

Teresa glanced at her watch. If this was what people referred to as Puerto Rican time, she could live without it. She drew a firm, straight line across the top of the page, followed by a second one right under it. If the girl didn't arrive in the next five minutes, she'd leave.

She let out a long breath. Maybe this whole trip to Puerto Rico was a big mistake. Maybe she was wasting her time. The chances for success with a reluctant client were minimal, to say the least. And when the client was a reluctant teenager, it only added to the challenge. She forced herself to relax. No sense getting all worked up. It never helped, and it always harmed.

Better to pray.

She bowed her head and closed her eyes. "Father, I'm here at Your direction. At least, I think I am. Please give me wisdom to handle Pilar's coaching in the way You would have me handle it. Please grant me favor with her, Father, so that her heart will receive what You want to give her through me. Thank You, Father. In Jesus' Name I pray. Amen."

A slight knock on the door triggered a rush of adrenaline. Teresa lifted her gaze and forced a smile. "Come in, Pilar," she called.

The door opened slightly. Shy and timid, Pilar stood in the doorway.

Teresa motioned with her hand. "Come in. I've been waiting for you." *For ten long minutes.*

At the sight of the young girl's sullen face, Teresa's heart softened. She rose and motioned Pilar toward the sofa then closed the door. "Let's sit here. It will be more comfortable for both of us."

The young teen took the spot at the far end of the sofa and pressed tightly into its side, head bowed, eyes lowered, and arms crossed tightly across her chest.

Teresa sighed. *The perfect attitude for a successful coaching session.* She sat on the other end of the sofa and breathed a silent prayer for wisdom then folded her hands on her lap. "So, I know you don't want to be here." Better to confront the negative head-on.

Pilar responded with a sidelong glance. "How did you know?"

Teresa chuckled. "It doesn't take much to figure it out. A hanging head and crossed arms don't usually mean you're excited about life. Besides, if I were you, I wouldn't want to be here either." Her training kicked in. *Shock them with empathy.*

"You wouldn't?" The child shifted and relaxed her arms slightly.

"Nope. I don't like being told what to do. Especially when it's my parent doing the telling." Teresa measured her words against Pilar's reactions. Searching for clues. Reading her body language. "Just before I left to come here, my mother scolded me for not eating enough. Would you believe it? And I, a grown woman." Teresa smiled at the memory. "So, I understand what it's like to have your Dad tell you you have to be coached. Against your wishes."

Pilar laughed. A small, nervous laugh, but it was a beginning.

An entry point into her soul.

Teresa's heart grew lighter. "So, tell me. What else does your father make you do?"

Pilar quirked her mouth. "He makes me eat string beans, and I hate string beans."

"String beans, eh? So that's where my mother gets it. Must be a Puerto Rican thing. That's exactly what she hammers me about all the time."

Pilar tilted her head and twisted a long strand of her light brown hair. "I wish I had a mother to hammer me about things."

A lump caught in Teresa's throat. Her training rushed back to her, like the reflex action when one slams on the breaks while driving. Proceed carefully with the soul of another. It's holy ground. Tread gently. "Do you know anything about your mother?"

Pilar folded her arms more tightly and pressed them against her chest, remaining in that position for a long moment. "Only that she was beautiful. My father and grandmother have lots of pictures of her."

"Do you look like her?"

"A little, I think. My eyes are shaped like hers, but

my hair is lighter."

Teresa studied the girl's face. Despite the signs of burgeoning womanhood, it still retained the tender lines of childhood. "Do you know anything else about your mother? Things your father and grandmother have told you?"

Pilar curled her shoulders forward and drew up her legs, as though reverting to a fetal position. A definite sign of stress and emotional pain.

Teresa backed off. Her goal as a coach was to move her client forward, not backward. But sometimes moving forward meant going backward to sever emotional chains that kept one from advancing.

It was time to change the subject so as not to lose ground. Too much probing too soon could end in loss of confidence and failed coaching. "Do you have any close friends at school?"

"Only one. Luisa."

"Have you known her long?"

"Since we were six years old." Pilar shifted in her seat and yawned. "Do you mind if we end our session now? I have some homework to do."

The girl's comment kindled Teresa's ire. An ire she forced herself to control. "Why do you want to end now? We've just gotten started. Besides, your father has paid for an hour session, so I want to give him his money's worth."

"But I told Papa I didn't want to be coached. He promised me if I tried it and didn't like it, I could stop."

Why hadn't Marcos alerted her to that promise before she made the trip from New Jersey?

Teresa took in a deep breath. Perhaps switching tactics would encourage Pilar to remain. "So, you don't like coaching?"

"No. I don't like it at all."

"What don't you like about it?"

"I don't like the questioning. I feel as though I'm on

a witness stand."

Teresa back-pedaled. Time to regain her footing. "Okay. I get it." She proffered a smile. "Now it's your turn."

"My turn for what?"

"To question me."

Pilar stared at her. "That's weird."

"What's weird about it?"

"I'm not a coach. I wouldn't even know what questions to ask you."

Teresa smiled. "You can ask me anything you want, as long as you don't ask me about why I hate string beans. Fair enough?"

Pilar broke into a tentative smile. "I don't know." The girl moved to the edge of the sofa. "I still think I want to leave. I have tons of homework to do." She got up. "I don't mean to be rude or anything."

Teresa considered her options. Forcing Pilar to stay would violate all coaching protocol and simple human decency. "Well, I can't force you to stay. Do you want to try another session later? Maybe when you've finished your homework?"

Pilar walked toward the door. "I don't think so. I'll just tell my Dad things didn't work out." She took hold of the doorknob. "Thanks, anyway." She left, closing the door behind her.

Teresa leaned back against the sofa and closed her eyes. So much for her good intentions. Was the girl a spoiled brat? A child who had her father wrapped around her little finger? Or was she really a teen with serious issues who needed help? If the latter, then maybe Teresa was the wrong person to help her. It was obvious Pilar hadn't taken to her. Maybe Marcos should find someone else to help his daughter.

Teresa had a sudden urge to pack up and leave. What was she thinking when she'd accepted Ramona's invitation? That she who could not help herself could help anyone else? Let alone a troubled teen?

Her insides coiled into a tight knot. Perhaps she'd been too pushy. Too probing. She should have proceeded more slowly, more tactfully. Maybe she wasn't as good with kids as she thought she was. Maybe she'd refused to recognize her limits in agreeing to help Pilar.

Her mind drifted to Roberto. They'd hoped to have a child of their own someday. But with Roberto's death, that dream had died, too. And now, after her brilliant session with Pilar, did she even have what it took to deal with children?

She rose from the couch and walked toward the window. It overlooked the back garden of the inn, a lush oasis blazing with color in the afternoon sun. Her gaze scanned the beautiful red and yellow hibiscus flowers, fully open to the brilliant sun. They seemed happy in a way she might never be happy again. What was their secret?

They trust in Me.

The Lord's loving conviction touched her spirit. Was that her problem? Was she not trusting God for her future? Was she trusting only herself?

She started to turn away when Marcos' head appeared above a purple hydrangea bush. Her heart lurched. She'd failed him, too. When he learned of her miserable session with Pilar, he'd be disappointed. She'd refund his money. It was the least she could do to make amends.

Before she could turn away, his eyes found her, mesmerizing her with their intensity even at a distance. Her heart quickened.

He waved at her and smiled.

Her face aflame, she quickly turned away, grabbed her purse, and left the office. This would not do. This simply would not do. Perhaps she should shorten her stay and return to New Jersey. Somehow it was easier to keep focused on Roberto's memory there. She wasn't surrounded by this tropical beauty, this relaxing lifestyle.

This sensitive man who, in spite of her resolve, was making inroads into her heart against her will.

She headed toward her suite, all the while trying to calm the pounding within her.

Did Marcos think she'd been searching for him? If so, how embarrassing!

She placed her purse strap on her shoulder.

In the future, she'd stay away from windows.

* * *

Marcos laid down his gardening clippers and headed toward the inn. Strange. Teresa was supposed to be in the middle of a coaching session with Pilar. Why, then, was she standing at the window? Was Pilar giving her trouble? He'd take care of that right away. Pilar would treat Teresa with respect, or else.

His muscles tense, he took the back steps two at a time and opened the screen door, letting it slam shut behind him. As he rounded the hallway, he nearly collided with Teresa. "Oh, Teresa. I'm so sorry." He paused, wishing he could take her in his arms. "What are you doing here? I thought you were having a session with Pilar."

Teresa stopped and folded her arms. "I was, but she told me she didn't want to be coached."

His insides churned. "She told you what?"

"That she didn't want to be coached. That you said if she tried it and didn't like it, she could stop."

A look of guilt crossed Marcos' face. "I did. I'm sorry. Not a good move on my part."

Teresa dismissed her irritation with him. "Well, it's over and done with."

"Did you insist she stay?"

"Marcos, the coaching relationship is a purely

47

voluntary one on both sides. If a client doesn't want to be coached, there's nothing I can do but comply with the client's wishes."

Marcos raked his fingers through his hair. "Can we talk? I've got to understand what's going on."

She nodded, and he pointed toward a small alcove at the far end of the hallway where they could talk privately.

As Teresa walked past him to take her seat, the scent of her perfume wafted against his nostrils, exciting his desire.

He waited for her to be seated then took the chair next to hers. "What happened?"

"The session started out on the wrong foot. Pilar arrived ten minutes late. I could tell by her body language that she was not at all happy to be there. I made small talk to break the ice. At first, she seemed to open up, but then she suddenly decided she wanted to leave. Said she had a lot of homework to do. I offered to coach her after she finished her homework, but she declined. She let me know in so many words she was done with coaching."

He rubbed his hands together. "That girl has me baffled. She's never been a rebellious child. What do you think is going on?"

"I think it has to do with her mother."

"What makes you think that?"

Teresa looked squarely at him. "She made a telling comment. When I mentioned that my mother hammers me about eating string beans, Pilar said she wished she had a mother to hammer her."

Marcos's heart clenched. "So that's the issue." He drew in a deep breath. "Marguerita."

"Marguerita?"

"Yes. Marguerita was my late wife's name."

"I see."

He swallowed hard at the memory of his deceased

wife and Pilar's mother. A woman like her graced the earth only once in each generation. She was the essence of life itself. Her every deed, her every word, her every look gave life. Yet, death had snatched her in the very act of giving life to the fruit of their love. Their precious child. Pilar. "Can we discuss this more at dinner? Right now, I need to talk with Pilar and then take care of some guest arrivals."

"Very well. I'll meet you in the dining room this evening."

Marcos rose as she did. "Until then."

Teresa nodded then turned to go.

He watched her leave. For the first time since Marguerita's death, his heart wanted to call out to a woman.

* * *

Teresa shut the door of her suite. Fatigue settled over her like a gray fog. Not physical fatigue, but the emotional fatigue that marks a deep sense of failure. She flopped across the bed. Maybe a nap would do her good. She hadn't slept well the night before. New country. New bed. New client. The lack of sleep had now caught up with her. She set the alarm clock for 5:00 pm, drew the pillow toward her, and placed her face upon it. In a few moments, she entered the sweet oblivion of sound sleep.

At the buzz of the alarm clock, she awakened from her nap. After her challenging session with Pilar, sleep had beckoned as a hiding place from discouragement. A practice she'd been engaging in far too much lately. She smiled wryly. Maybe she needed a life coach.

She lay in bed for a while longer. The late afternoon sun filtered through the drawn gauze curtains of her bedroom, lending a soft, warm glow to the hand-embroidered coverlet.

She glanced at the clock. Five-eleven p.m. Dinner

would be served at six.

And dinner meant seeing Marcos again.

By now, he must have already spoken with Pilar and learned of the fiasco of their first session. Teresa's chest tightened. What more could she say to him? She should have tried a different technique with Pilar. Maybe remained a little more distant at first, less probing, until the girl warmed up to her.

She threw off the coverlet and sat on the edge of the bed, trying to gather her thoughts. Reaching for her robe on the nearby chair, she rose and headed for the bathroom to freshen up.

The sudden jangling of the telephone startled her.

"Hello."

"Teresa, this is Marcos." His voice was like warm oil caressing her soul.

She switched to cautious mode. "Marcos." Why did the sound of his name on her lips trouble her in such a pleasant way? "Did you speak with Pilar? I'm so sorry about what happened."

"I've reserved a table for us in the back of the dining room. We can talk privately there."

His failure to respond to her apology unnerved her. Was he angry? Disappointed?

Upset?

She clenched the telephone. "Yes. I plan to be there at six."

"Okay. See you then."

The line clicked shut before she could reply.

Her self-confidence clicked shut, too.

Chapter Six

Marcos ended the call to Teresa. This was no time to allow his emotions to get out of hand. He must remain focused on Pilar and on Teresa's single purpose in coming to Puerto Rico. Frankly, he hadn't expected to be so taken with Marisol's daughter. Indeed, he hadn't expected to be taken at all.

But meeting Teresa had blown him away. Yet, it wasn't only her beauty. Puerto Rico was full of beautiful women—extraordinarily beautiful ones. But none had captured his heart as had Teresa. Her beauty was not only outward, but also inward. There was a sense of confident serenity about her that calmed his troubled soul. Hers were still waters that ran deep.

He drew in a long breath. He must not—would not—allow his own feelings to enter into Pilar's coaching situation. Not only would it be grossly unprofessional, but it would also be detrimental to Pilar's progress. Especially since she obviously did not care for Teresa.

He glanced at his wristwatch. Five-fourteen pm. He had forty-five minutes before meeting Teresa in the dining room. Enough time to talk to his Lord then shower and dress for dinner.

A dinner he hoped would bring peace to his troubled soul.

Mamá stopped him on his way to the dining room. "So, how are things going with the coaching?"

Of course, she meant with Teresa. "Not so well."

"What do you mean, 'not so well'?"

"Pilar is giving us a hard time." Marcos glanced at

his watch. "Can we talk about this later, Mamá? I'm scheduled to meet Teresa for dinner in five minutes."

The corners of Ramona's lips turned up into a broad grin. "Speaking of dinner, please tell Teresa that I would like to host her myself with a traditional Puerto Rican dinner in my apartment on Friday evening."

Marcos smiled. "She would love that."

"We need to expose her to our Puerto Rican culture while she's here. In fact, why don't the two of you take the day off tomorrow so you can give her the grand tour of Old San Juan?"

If he weren't in such a hurry, he'd give Mamá a piece of his mind for playing the yenta. But because he didn't want to be late for dinner with Teresa, he simply nodded and pointed to his wristwatch, tapping it several times for emphasis.

"Go on," Mamá said, pushing him out of the lobby. "First things first."

He gave her a quick peck on the cheek and broke into a jog on his way to the dining room.

* * *

Upon entering the cozy dining room, Teresa spotted Marcos seated at a small table at the far corner of the room. His back was toward her. Was it a sign that he was upset with her? That he was preparing to fire her?

She'd resign first.

Teresa crossed the dining room and approached his table. "*Hola*, Marcos." The tremor in her voice betrayed the roiling in her stomach.

He looked up, stood, and smiled at her. "*Hola*, Teresa. Please, sit down." He motioned toward the chair opposite him.

Holding her purse close to her chest, she slid into the empty chair then placed her purse on the floor at her feet.

He waited for her to be settled before taking his seat.

"Marcos, I want to apologize—"

He lifted a palm. "No need to apologize, Teresa. You're right on time."

She gave him a questioning look. "Excuse me?"

"You're right on time. I'm the one who was concerned about being late."

She laughed. "No, I meant I want to apologize about the fiasco with Pilar's coaching session today."

"It's not your fault." Weariness edged his voice.

"But I should have used a different approach. Maybe if I hadn't asked so many questions upfront. Maybe if I'd allowed her more time to warm up to me."

Marcos shook his head. "No. It's not that at all. I'm sure of it. Pilar is simply being stubborn."

The maternal instinct resident in woman rose up within her. "But, Marcos. She's hurting. And hurting very deeply."

His gaze met hers head-on. "I'm sure she's hurting, but that's no excuse for poor manners. She treated you badly when she first met you, and now she leaves in the middle of a coaching session?" He shook his head again. "No. I will not tolerate it. I did not train her to do such things."

It would do no good to retort. Marcos, it was obvious, was as stubborn as he judged his daughter to be. "Very well, then. But I do not agree with the way you want to handle the situation. If you punish her, you will simply drive her away, and she'll withdraw into herself even more."

His face softened, and he smiled. "I like a woman who pushes back a little. Who doesn't readily agree with whatever I say."

Heat flooded Teresa's face. His compliment took

53

her by surprise. To her great dismay, by pleasant surprise.

He placed his elbows on the table and leaned forward. "So, what do you suggest I do?"

His question drew her in with its urgency. "Marcos, Pilar is displaying the symptoms of a child who is still grieving over the loss of her mother."

Marcos remained silent, his face taut with pain.

Instinctively, Teresa placed her hand on his, then quickly withdrew it, but not before a spark of life flew from his hand to hers.

He exhaled a long breath. "So that is the real issue. Not having a mother."

"Yes, but it's more than that. Lots of children don't have mothers but manage to lead normal lives. There's something more going on here. Something beyond not having a mother."

"What do you think it is?"

Teresa drew in a deep breath. "This is just a hunch, but hunches are often true." She measured her words. "I think Pilar is blaming herself for her mother's death."

Marcos rubbed a hand across his forehead. "Lord, have mercy! But why?"

"Because she knows Marguerita died in childbirth."

"But women occasionally die in childbirth."

"Yes, but when the woman is your mother, matters become much more personal."

Marcos shook his head. "No child should have to bear such a burden."

"I agree. So let's find out if my hunch is right."

Marcos shifted uncomfortably in his chair. "But how?"

"Just ask her."

"That's easier said than done."

"What do you mean?"

"Whenever I mention Marguerita, Pilar breaks down and cries."

"So, my hunch may be right."

"Yes, it may be."

Teresa studied the lines around his eyes. "I know this is difficult for you, but we have to get to the bottom of things in order to help Pilar." She had an overpowering desire to comfort him. She leaned forward in her chair. "The only way to find out if Pilar is blaming herself is to ask her."

Marcos' eyes met hers. They were liquid with pain, penetrating the depths of her soul. "I will do whatever I have to do to help my child."

A warm sensation flooded Teresa's heart. This was a humble man, a good man, a hurting man. She wanted to help him as well as his daughter.

"Grieving is a strange thing." Marcos let out a long breath. "It lingers longer than one expects and rises to the surface again long after one thinks it's over."

Lingers longer than one expects. Yes. That's exactly what had happened with Roberto. But, truth be told, Teresa never expected her grief for Roberto to end.

Maybe that was the reason it hadn't.

Ending grief meant ending love. Or did it?

Marcos leaned toward her, his breath warming her face. "So what is our next step with Pilar?"

Teresa did not miss the word *our*. "Your next step is to ask her if she is blaming herself for her mother's death."

A worried look crossed Marcos' face. "To be honest, I'm afraid of her reaction." He hesitated. "She may fall apart. Or, worse yet, burst into a rage." He furrowed his brows. "Would it be too much for me to ask you to be present?"

Teresa prayed a silent prayer for wisdom. "It's best if you talk with her alone since this involves your wife and her mother."

Marcos lowered his gaze. "You're right. I'll talk with her this evening."

She studied his face. "If you and Pilar would like to talk with me afterward, just call me."

He nodded and broke into a smile. "By the way, Mamá wants to invite you to her apartment for a traditional Puerto Rican dinner on Friday evening."

"That would be lovely."

He cleared his throat and gave her a sheepish grin. "And she also suggested I give you the grand tour of Old San Juan."

Teresa's stomach tensed. She'd never been out alone with a man since Roberto's death. But it would be rude to refuse the son of her mother's best friend.

"You can't go back to New Jersey without having seen beautiful Old San Juan."

He must have sensed her hesitancy. If she delayed any longer in responding, she would appear rude for sure. She would not offend him—nor Ramona—by refusing his invitation. "Yes, I would love to tour Old San Juan with one of her natives."

"Wonderful! Let's do it tomorrow. You need a day off, and we both need time to discuss what to do about Pilar."

Her mind wrestled with her heart. What would Roberto think? Would she be betraying him by spending the day with another man? Would she be guilty of infidelity?

"So, is it a date for tomorrow?" Marcos smiled, a smile that held hope and promise.

A smile that touched her deeply even though she didn't want to be touched.

"Well?"

She smiled in return. "It's a date." The words came with great difficulty. But they came.

Marcos exhaled in mock relief. "And now, dear Teresa, I think it's time to have some dinner."

With that, he called for the waiter.

But Teresa had lost her appetite.

* * *

Upon entering his apartment, Marcos found Pilar stretched out on the sofa, watching TV. She acknowledged him with a curt "hola" and kept her eyes glued on the TV screen.

Marcos sat down in a chair across from the sofa. "What are you watching?"

"A movie."

"Which movie?"

"*Facing the Giants*."

"Good movie."

Pilar flicked off the TV. "I've watched it a dozen times. There's nothing better to do."

Marcos stretched out his legs and folded his hands. "So, how was your first coaching session?"

"Boring."

"Boring? Why?"

"She just asked me a lot of stupid questions."

"What do you mean stupid questions?"

Pilar folded her arms across her chest. "I mean stupid questions."

Marcos' muscles tensed. "Can you give me an example of one of the stupid questions Dr. Gonzalez asked you?"

Pilar thought a moment. "She asked me who my best friend is."

"What's so stupid about that question?"

"My best friend has nothing to do with my problem."

Marcos tried with all his might not to raise his voice. "What *does* have to do with your problem, Pilar? Would you please tell me?" He was on his last nerve.

She unfolded her arms and dropped them to her lap.

"I don't know, Papa. I feel like a pile of tangled emotions. I don't know where one starts and the other ends."

"Then why won't you let Dr. Gonzalez help you? She's trained in helping people untangle their emotions."

Pilar remained silent.

"Pilar, please. Tell me what's wrong. Is it that you don't like Dr. Gonzalez?"

"No. I like her a lot."

"Then why won't you talk with her?"

"I don't know, Papa. I guess I feel embarrassed."

"Embarrassed about what?"

"About having a problem."

Marcos crossed the room and sat by his daughter. "Pilar, it's not shameful to have a problem. It's shameful not to try to solve the problem."

She didn't respond. She only stared into.space.

Should he bring up the topic of Marguerita? Teresa's advice that he ask Pilar if she blamed herself for her mother's death was right, but difficult. Even in his own mind, remembering the event stirred up old feelings of anger toward God at taking his wife. Feelings that, if he were honest with himself, he hadn't yet truly resolved.

The memory of that horrible night still churned in his soul. At the first sign of labor, he'd rushed Marguerita to the hospital. Her blood pressure had risen to dangerous heights. Doctors feared toxemia. Marcos still remembered the frightened look on her face. The perspiration on her brow.

The panic in her voice.

He wiped her forehead with a damp cloth, attempting to calm her while his own soul trembled. "It will be all right, Marguerita. Don't worry."

But it didn't turn out all right at all. In the process of giving Pilar life, his beloved wife lost her own.

When Marguerita died, he died with her.

Tears stung his eyes. Maybe now wasn't the right

time to broach the subject with Pilar.
But would there ever be a right time?

Chapter Seven

The next morning, Teresa awoke at the crack of dawn. Her guilty conscience balked at the prospect of spending the day with Marcos, yet her heart stirred with anticipation. What was wrong? She'd heard of misinformed consciences, consciences beset by scrupulosity because of wrong perceptions of God's Word. Did she have such a conscience? If so, was it keeping her from moving on with her life?

She lay looking at the ceiling. What did it mean to "forget those things that are behind," as the Apostle Paul taught in the Book of Philippians? Did it mean to forget Roberto altogether? Did it mean to bury her wonderful memories of him? Or did it simply mean to stop living in a past that no longer existed in order to live in a present that did?

Perhaps Mamá was right. Dear Mamá who'd never finished high school but was wiser than many with a string of degrees after their names. Teresa needed to lay aside the past and move forward with her life. After all, isn't that what Roberto would have wanted her to do?

Yet, the inner conflict remained, although being around Marcos was causing its hold on her to weaken. Was that a good thing or not?

She sat up on the side of the bed and stretched. A narrow ribbon of sunshine filtered through the cream-colored curtains and draped itself across the room. Outside her window, a warbler chirped wildly, in praise to the God Who created it.

Teresa stood and walked toward the French doors that led to the deck. She opened them to allow the fresh salt breeze to enter her room. How life-giving it felt as it filled her expanding lungs! In the distance, the whitecaps of the Atlantic lapped rhythmically against the sandy shore, while the last purple shadows of night slipped quickly behind the morning sun.

A sense of deep connection to this land overwhelmed her. Her roots lay in this beautiful paradise. She'd been conceived here and birthed here, not only physically but also emotionally, culturally, and psychologically. Her very identity lay in this beautiful corner of the earth called Puerto Rico.

Yet, her life was in New Jersey. It was there her parents had brought her in the hope of finding a better life for their then five-year-old daughter. By God's grace, they had found that better life, and Teresa had reaped the blessings of it. Soon she would be returning to that life.

So, why all of a sudden did she not want to leave?

The alarm clock on the nightstand sounded, jolting her from her thoughts.

Six-fifteen a.m. Marcos would be meeting her in the lobby at eight, and then they'd be off for the grand tour of Old San Juan. She'd best get ready.

She grabbed her robe and headed to the shower. She'd laid out her clothes the night before, so all the major decisions about what to wear had been made. She'd chosen a navy blue pant suit with a white tank top and white sandals. She smiled. New Jersey was under a blanket of snow. She'd have to wait six or seven more months at least to don this outfit back home.

After dressing, putting on her makeup, and spending time with the Lord in Bible reading and prayer, Teresa hastened to the lobby where Marcos would be waiting. A bubbling Ramona greeted her.

"Teresita!" Ramona gave her a warm hug. "How are you enjoying your stay with us?"

"I'm enjoying it immensely. The atmosphere is so

warm and inviting, and your hospitality surpasses even that of five-star hotels."

Ramona laughed. "Thank you. It's Holy Spirit's presence in our midst. We call it the *Inn of the Dove* for a reason." Her eyes twinkled. "We do our best to make our inn feel like a home-away-from-home to our guests."

"Well, you certainly have achieved your goal and more."

"Come, sit down." Ramona motioned Teresa to a nearby sofa and sat beside her. "I hear that Marcos is going to give you the grand tour of Old San Juan today."

Heat flooded Teresa's cheeks. "Yes. He's very kind to take a day off to shuffle me around when I could tour the city myself."

"Absolutely not! Marcos wouldn't think of it. Part of our Puerto Rican hospitality is to show family and friends our beautiful city. We give them an inside view they can't get any other way."

Teresa's heart warmed.

"By the way." Ramona took Teresa's hand. "Did Marcos tell you I want to have you to my apartment for a traditional Puerto Rican dinner on Friday evening? Or at some point before you leave?"

"Yes, thank you so very much, especially since I will be leaving soon."

Surprise crossed Ramona's face. "Soon?"

"Unfortunately, yes. Pilar doesn't seem open to the coaching process, and if a client is reluctant, there isn't much I can do to help."

Ramona furrowed her brows and patted Teresa's arm. "I will speak with Pilar myself." Ramona leaned into Teresa. "Between you and me," she lowered her voice to almost a whisper, "a grandparent has an influence a parent does not."

Teresa remembered her own grandmother who'd moved with them to the States but had died only a short time thereafter. *Abuela* had a way of convincing Teresa that even the most unpleasant task could be a lot of fun if laughter and song accompanied it. "I fully understand, Ramona. My grandmother was a lot like you."

"Ah, Marcos!" Ramona turned toward her son who had just entered the lobby. "There you are. You have been keeping this beautiful lady waiting far too long." She winked at him.

Marcos turned a dark shade of crimson and looked at his watch. "Actually, Mamá, I'm right on time." He then turned to Teresa and smiled. "Are you ready to see the sights of Old San Juan?"

The white polo shirt he wore complemented his olive skin and accentuated the blue of his eyes. Eyes that were like clear pools, allowing her to see deep into his soul. She stopped her heart before it fell in.

"Yes, I'm ready." She picked up her purse and rose.

Marcos offered her his arm. "Then we shall be on our way." He turned toward Mamá. "Please keep an eye on Pilar. We'll be back after dinner, around nine p.m."

"Don't you worry about Pilar. I'll take care of everything. Just have fun."

Arm tucked in his, Teresa followed Marcos out of the lobby, across the wide, hibiscus-laden porch, and down to his navy blue Toyota. He opened the passenger door and waited for her to get in. As she fastened her seatbelt across her body, she wavered about fastening the seatbelt on her heart.

* * *

Marcos rolled down his window to catch a breath of the fresh salt breeze. He couldn't have picked a better day to escort Teresa around Old San Juan. The sky was a cloudless blue, the blue of robin eggs. The temperature was a comfortable eighty-two degrees, and the air was dry, unusual for San Juan. Best of all, the company was perfect.

He drove the car around the circular driveway in front of the Inn and onto the road that led to the main highway. Tall palm trees lined the road, their lovely fronds swaying in the gentle breeze that carried the fragrance of hibiscus, bougainvillea, and roses.

He glanced at Teresa. "Are you excited about seeing the city of your roots?" The sunlight danced on her long brown hair like so many twinkling lights. He wanted to dance with it and feel the vibrations of its music between his fingers.

"Very excited. Actually, I was born just outside of San Juan, across the bay in a little town called Cataño, where my father was working at the time."

"I know Cataño. It's a charming town. Would you like to take a side trip there?"

"Yes, if we have time."

He smiled. "We'll make time. It's only an eight-minute ride by ferry. You'll love it."

"Mamá used to tell me how charming it is."

"Let's explore Old San Juan first, have lunch, and then head over to Cataño."

Teresa's delight was like balm to his empty soul.

"You're the tour guide. I'm just the tourist."

"So, when did your parents move to Old San Juan?"

"Shortly after I was born. Mamá wanted to return to her native city, so when a job opening came up for my father, he moved the family back here. Eventually, we moved to the States." Teresa turned toward him. "How about you?"

Marcos entered the main highway and merged into traffic. "I was born right here in Old San Juan. This highway we're entering is the *Avenida Luis Muñoz Rivera*. It's the main highway in Old San Juan that caresses the shores of the Atlantic Ocean." He moved into the right lane for an unobstructed view. "Have you ever seen a more spectacular sight?" He pointed a finger in the direction of the ocean, but his gaze stopped short, his eyes lingering on Teresa as his throat tightened. Having her beside him felt so right. "Let's stop for a moment to take in the view." He pulled over to a small area designated a scenic spot. He got out of the car, went over to the passenger side, and opened the door for Teresa. "Let's walk to the water's edge." He wanted so much to take her hand, but he resisted the impulse.

They removed their shoes and stood on the shore, the waters of the Atlantic lapping at their bare feet. Marcos looked at her. "What do you think?"

"It's magnificent."

"Yes, it is." His eyes remained glued to her lovely face.

"And you get to live with this view day in and day out." The instant she turned toward him, his eyes locked on hers. He wanted to say she, too, could live with this view day in and day out—if only. His heart spun. Had he lost his mind? If only what? If only she became his wife? If only she'd agree to marry him? But that was entirely out of the question. He reined in his galloping emotions. It could never be. Teresa's life was in the States; his was here.

He swallowed hard. "We'd better get back on the road if we want to see the most important sites." But as Marcos studied her beautiful face riveted on the majestic Atlantic, he realized the most important sight he wanted to see was standing right in front of him.

* * *

Teresa slid back into the passenger seat and leaned back against the headrest. Being with Marcos stirred feelings long dormant within her soul. Feelings she'd thought had been buried with Roberto.

Feelings she feared.

66

She took in a deep breath and sighed.

Marcos slipped into the driver's seat and closed the door. "And now, on to Fort San Cristobal, just up the road a bit." He smiled, put the car in gear, and slowly entered the highway.

Teresa turned toward him. "Tell me about Fort San Cristobal."

"Fort San Cristobal is one of two forts that used to protect San Juan Harbor. The other is El Morro which we'll visit a little later. Fort San Cristobal was used by the United States Army as a military base during World War II."

"Interesting. I didn't know that." Teresa sat up.

Marcos nodded. "But after the US Army left in 1961, the fort became a part of the World Heritage Site under the auspices of the United Nations."

Teresa turned to him and smiled. "I'm impressed with your knowledge. Where did you learn all of this?"

He chuckled. "I'm a bit of a history buff. And, truth be told, I worked as a tour guide at Fort San Cristobal during my college years to help pay my tuition."

"Ah! So I have the great privilege of taking a tour with a professional tour guide. You're a modest man."

His face reddened. "Well, I wouldn't call myself a professional tour guide. Just a lover of my native city."

"In my opinion, anyone who used to give tours of Fort San Cristobal is a professional."

His glance was tender. "Thank you for the compliment."

Teresa's throat constricted. "You're welcome. Mamá always taught me to give credit where credit is due."

"The friendship between your mother and mine goes back a long way."

"Yes, Mamá said she met your mother in the first grade." Teresa smiled. "That's a long time to be friends."

"My mother spoke continually of Marisol during my growing up years. She would recount their adventures as schoolgirls. Mama's face always lit up when she spoke of your mother."

Teresa laughed. "I had the same experience when my mother spoke of yours."

"So, we also have our mothers in common."

Also. What was Marcos thinking? What else did he and she have in common? Dare she ask?

She ventured the question. "What else do we have in common?"

He turned toward her.

The look in his eyes startled her.

"We share a common pain." His voice was husky.

Teresa's stomach tightened. She turned her face toward the ocean. A common pain. Yes. Both she and Marcos had lost their spouses. Their life partners.

Their soul mates.

Yes. They did, indeed, share a common pain. She turned her gaze toward him. Toward his glistening eyes. "What was Marguerita like?"

He smiled. "I'll tell you if you promise to tell me what Roberto was like."

Somehow his simple request calmed her palpitating heart. "It's a deal."

For the next few miles, Marcos expounded on the virtues of his deceased wife, followed by Teresa and her litany of Roberto's virtues.

As they pulled into the parking lot of Fort San Cristobal, Marcos turned toward her. "But that's all in the past. It's time to move on with life, right?"

The way he looked at her sent chills down her spine. Why was he asking her this question? What did his moving on with life have to do with her own?

What was he thinking?

Marcos got out of the car and opened the passenger door. Extending his hand toward her, he helped her out of the car.

The only problem was he didn't let go of her hand after she got out of the car.

No. That wasn't the only problem. The other problem was she didn't want to withdraw her hand from his as they headed toward Fort San Cristobal.

But she did.

Chapter Eight

After a whirlwind day of visiting the key sites of San Juan—El Morro, the Cathedral of San Juan, and the Fine Arts Center— as well as a side trip to her birthplace of Cataño—Teresa welcomed the break for a leisurely dinner. The day had brought with it a multitude of conflicting emotions that, she feared, were making her vulnerable to lapses in judgment. She couldn't deny that being with Marcos filled her with a joy she hadn't experienced since Roberto's untimely death. But she also could not deny that experiencing that joy triggered deep guilt. Enjoying the company of any man besides Roberto smacked of infidelity to his memory.

But was she really thinking straight?

She didn't know anymore. The natural beauty of the place, the tropical atmosphere that appealed strongly to the senses, the presence of a man who inspired her confidence, not to mention who stirred her emotions, threatened to rob her of sound judgment and common sense. She needed some space to sort things out.

Marcos approached a luxurious hotel. "Here we are. The *La Concha* Renaissance Hotel. One of San Juan's finest. We're going to have dinner at *La Perla* Restaurant that sits in the back on the water's edge." He smiled at her.

Teresa looked up at the majestic hotel. It towered high against a purple-blue twilight sky.

"This is beautiful." She gazed in wonder at the amazing building before her.

He pulled into the circular driveway in front of the main entrance. "Wait till you see the restaurant." A valet approached the driver's side and opened the door for him.

Meanwhile a bellman opened Teresa's door and helped her out.

Marcos handed the valet the car keys and took the parking stub. He then turned to Teresa and offered her his arm. "Shall we?"

Against her will, her heart warmed. She smiled. "Yes."

They walked through the front doors of the hotel into a lobby that was at once beautiful yet functional. White leather sofas interspersed with white wicker chairs lined a lovely welcome area filled with the fragrance of lilies and roses. She spotted a restroom. "I'm going to freshen up a bit before we eat."

"Good idea. I'll meet you back here in a few minutes."

Teresa nodded. As she headed toward the ladies' room, she found herself walking with a lighter step.

And a lighter heart.

* * *

Marcos approached the men's room. Not since he'd first met Marguerita had he been so enthralled with a woman. Teresa was the answer to his every prayer. His every desire.

His every need.

But what if she didn't feel the same way about him?

Perhaps he was jumping the gun. Thinking only of himself and not of her.

He paused at the restroom sink and looked in the mirror, his eyes reflecting the deep emotions of his heart. Placing his trust in God, he bowed his head and prayed. "Father, You know my heart, and You know Your plans for me. Give me wisdom with Teresa. If she is the woman for me, confirm it for both of us, Lord. Open her heart to my love for her. In Jesus' Name. Amen."

* * *

When Teresa returned to the lobby, Marcos was already waiting for her. "Perfect timing. Our reservations are for six."

She looked at him in surprise. "You made reservations?"

"Of course. One must for *La Perla*. It's one of the most popular places for couples to dine."

She didn't miss his reference to them as a *couple*. Was Marcos thinking beyond a simple day together? A simple tour of his native city?

He led her to the back of the hotel where *La Perla* sat in all of its brilliant splendor. Shaped like a clamshell, the restaurant was not only an amazing architectural feat but also one of the most romantic places she'd ever seen. Edging the water, it offered a view that took her breath away.

A hostess greeted them. "Your name, please."

"Marcos Sanchez. Reservations for two for six o'clock."

The hostess checked the reservation list. "Yes. This way, please, Mr. and Mrs. Sanchez."

Teresa's breath caught. She glanced at Marcos. A bemused expression lined his face, accentuating the twinkle in his eyes.

She leaned into him and whispered. "Did you hear what she said?"

He smiled. "How could I miss it?"

"Aren't you going to correct her?"

"Why should I?"

Her temperature rose. "Why *shouldn't* you?"

"Because I don't see that any harm was done."

Teresa's stomach clenched. Why, the nerve!

The hostess reached a table for two by the waterfront. "At your request, Mr. Sanchez, we've given you and your wife the best table in the house. Enjoy."

"Thank you." As the hostess left, Marcos pulled out Teresa's chair. "Mrs. Sanchez?"

Teresa stiffened. Okay. It was time for the game to be over. "I'm sorry, Marcos, but I am not Mrs. Sanchez."

A look of sadness crossed his face. "Please forgive me. I didn't mean to offend you."

This was what happened when she dropped her guard. When she forgot to honor Roberto's memory.

When she succumbed to the needy feelings within her.

She straightened in her chair. "We need to talk about Pilar."

Marcos nodded. "Yes. You're right. Let's order first and then we'll talk while we eat."

Her stomach knotted. She'd wounded him. And for what reason? So as to maintain her dignity? Her resolve about Roberto?

Her pride?

What had so far proven to be a day of sweet communication was quickly turning into a sour exchange.

"Marcos, I'm sorry. I guess I'm too touchy about certain things. Like my husband's memory."

Compassion filled his gaze. "I understand. Roberto was very blessed to have had you as his wife."

Teresa's throat constricted. "Thank you for saying that."

He reached for her hand but then stopped. "You're welcome."

Good. She had the upper hand again. She'd regained control of her heart. Marcos knew exactly where she stood.

Teresa composed herself and studied the menu. "What do you recommend?"

"*La Perla* is known for its superb seafood dishes. The pollack with coconut curry is magnificent as is the pan-roasted sea bass."

Teresa's eyes scanned the many mouth-watering choices of seafood. Finally, she settled on the pollack with coconut curry.

Marcos smiled. "A good choice." The waiter approached their table to take their order.

Marcos spoke first. "The young lady will have the pollack with coconut curry, and I'll have the pan-roasted sea bass."

The waiter winked at Teresa. "A smart husband you have here, calling you a young lady."

Would the joking ever stop? Yet, she hadn't realized how much she'd missed having a gentleman order her dinner for her. Teresa's heart pounded. Maybe it was the view of the ocean waves lapping up against the restaurant; maybe it was the haunting sounds of the strolling violinist playing *Romanza de Amor*, the ever popular Spanish love song; maybe it was the nearness of Marcos' breath as he leaned toward her. Whatever it was, Teresa's heart wavered.

She inhaled a deep breath. "Let's talk about Pilar." She smiled. "After all, she's the reason I'm here." She shot him a warning glance, but it ricocheted. Whom was she kidding? The warning glance was for *her* heart, not his. He didn't seem to have a problem with holding on to the past.

Marcos leaned back in his chair. "Yes, let's talk about Pilar. I'm still angry about the way she disrespected you during her coaching session."

"It wasn't actually disrespect. She was very polite, but she just didn't want to finish the session."

He sat up. "Should I insist on the coaching?"

"That's a difficult question to answer. As her father, you have the right to insist. But insisting could backfire. She could be there physically but not emotionally. I noted a bit of a passive-aggressive tendency in her, which means she could say one thing on the surface but be thinking another underneath the surface."

"But Pilar doesn't lie."

"It's not lying exactly. It's a determination to do what one wants while pretending to comply with the rules."

"Just as I said. It's lying."

Teresa had to agree Marcos was right. His integrity inspired her deep admiration. He reminded her of Roberto. Uncompromising in his stance for truth. "Very well. I'll concede that. But I'm sure it's not her intention to lie. She's just trying to protect herself."

"From what?"

Teresa studied Marcos' face. Worry lined his eyes. His gaze, fixed on her, probed for answers. "From having to face what she thinks is her responsibility for her mother's death."

The waiter came with their meals. "Pollack with coconut curry for the Mrs. and pan-seared bass for the gentleman. Enjoy." The waiter gave a slight bow and left.

Whatever. This was no time to worry about an honest mistake in relationship. Pilar's problem was far more serious. "I think you need to encourage Pilar to continue with the coaching. I'll stay for the rest of the month, unless she comes around. We have three weeks left. Let's see what we can accomplish in three weeks."

Marcos nodded. "As soon as I get home, I'll tell Pilar that unless she resumes coaching, she will not be permitted to go to summer camp with our church youth group in July. That camping trip is the highlight of her year."

"Good. I'll schedule her for a session every afternoon after school at four o'clock. That will give us fifteen sessions before I return to New Jersey." Even as she said it, Teresa's heart resisted the thought of leaving this wonderful place.

Or was it really the thought of leaving this wonderful man?

Chapter Nine

After walking Teresa to her suite, Marcos returned to his own apartment. Despite several hours of exploring the sites of San Juan, his pace was light and his step was sure. Spending time with Teresa had only strengthened and confirmed the nascent feelings in his heart. She was the answer to his prayer. The woman God had provided to be his wife and the mother of his child.

Now, the only problem that remained was to convince Teresa.

He entered his apartment and found Pilar curled up with a book, waiting for him.

"You look happy." She closed the book in anticipation of his response.

He sat down and smiled. "I am happy. I just spent the day giving Teresa—Dr. Gonzalez—the grand tour of San Juan."

"I would think you'd be exhausted."

Marcos laughed. "One can be exhausted and happy at the same time."

Pilar drew her feet to her chest. "Did you talk about me?"

The muscles in Marcos' stomach tensed. "Yes, we did. A lot."

Pilar squirmed in her corner of the sofa.

"As a matter of fact, both Teresa—Dr. Gonzalez—and I strongly believe you should resume coaching."

"But I don't want to, Papa."

"Pilar, listen to me. You're not a baby who cannot reason. So please reason with me. Dr. Gonzalez believes she can help you, but she needs your cooperation. She came here all the way from New Jersey to help you. Does that mean anything to you?"

Pilar lowered her head. "Are you trying to put me on a guilt trip?"

Marcos sighed and slapped his hands on his knees. "No, Pilar. I'm not trying to put you on a guilt trip. I just want you to understand how much Teresa cares about you. Enough to come such a long way to help you."

"But she doesn't even know me. Why would she care about me?"

"Maybe it has something to do with general human compassion. But there is a bit more to it. Teresa's mother and my mother were the best of childhood friends. There is a bond between them that, in a way, includes Teresa and me, their children. And because you are my child, that bond includes you as well."

"I don't get it."

Marcos chuckled. "You don't have to get it, Sweetheart. Just trust me, okay?"

Pilar wrapped her arms around her knees. "So, what do you want me to do?"

"I want you to give coaching another chance. Teresa came for three months, but unless you're willing to cooperate with her, she'll return to New Jersey at the end of the first month."

The look on Pilar's face revealed her surprise. "She'll leave if I stop coaching? I thought she was here on vacation."

"Pilar, where have you been?" He shook his head. "Yes, Teresa came here just for you."

Pilar grew pensive. "All right, then. I'll let her coach me."

Marcos' muscles relaxed. "That's my girl." He got

up to give her a hug. "I knew you'd eventually come around."

Now, if he could only convince Pilar to accept Teresa not only as her coach, but also as her mother.

* * *

Moonbeams fell across the bed as Teresa lay on the coverlet, unable to go to sleep. She watched them cascade across the room, like liquid light caressing the atmosphere as they slid across the floor.

The bedside clock showed 11:39 p.m., but her body still vibrated with energy. Despite the heaviness of their conversation, the day she'd spent with Marcos touring San Juan had invigorated her. Filled her with a joy she didn't know was still possible.

Yet a joy that filled her with guilt. A guilt that seemed to be dissolving day by tropical day.

She'd better tighten her guard.

Marcos was a man of great heart and deep emotion.

An emotion she feared, not because of its depth but because of its object. He was falling in love with her. Perhaps had already fallen in love with her. She recognized the familiar look in his eye. The same look Roberto had had when he'd asked her to marry him.

But the fact Marcos might be falling in love with her was not the problem. The problem was she might be falling in love with Marcos.

Despite the warmth of the night, a shiver ran through her.

She turned over and pounded her pillow before burying her face in it. No. She could not let this happen. She *would* not let this happen.

But while her will insisted, her heart fought to over-rule her will.

What was it she'd learned in coaching training?

When the head and the heart are in conflict, the heart will always win out?

She drew in a deep breath. She would guard her heart. She would keep it locked no matter how much Marcos tried to unlock it.

She turned over on her back and stared at the ceiling. The only solution was to return to New Jersey. To the place where Roberto's grave would be a constant reminder of her pledge to remain faithful to him.

To the place where his presence permeated her surroundings.

To the place where she would not have to face herself.

* * *

The next morning, Teresa welcomed Pilar to her office right on time. *We're off to a good start.* "Good morning, Pilar."

"Good morning, Dr. Gonzalez."

Teresa smiled. "You can call me Teresa if you wish." She motioned Pilar to join her on the sofa.

"I feel strange doing that." Pilar sat down at the far end of the sofa.

"No problem. I'm glad you decided to resume coaching."

Pilar only nodded.

Teresa pursed her lips. Was Pilar resisting her again, or was she just nervous? "How are things going at school?"

"Okay."

"Just okay?"

"Yeah. Just okay."

Teresa studied the child's body language. Her arms tightly crossed her chest, indicating Pilar was shutting her out. Protecting herself.

"Pilar, please tell me the truth. Are you here

because you want to be here, or are you here because your father coerced you to come?"

"What does *coerced* mean?"

"It means *forced*. Did your father force you to come?"

"No." She lowered her eyes. "I mean, he didn't actually force me." She hesitated. "He told me you came all the way to San Juan just for me, and it would be rude not to let you coach me."

Teresa considered Pilar's words. "So, you're here because you don't want to be rude."

"Uh-huh."

"Are you at all here because you want to get better?"

Pilar shook her head. "No. Not really."

"Do you want to get better?"

"I'm not sure I know what you mean. Papa thinks I'm depressed. Yeah, I'm sad a lot, but I don't think I'm all that bad."

"Are you willing to spend the next three weeks working on your sadness?" If Pilar did not respond to coaching within three weeks, Teresa would return to the States.

"I guess so."

"I need more than an 'I guess so.' I need a firm *yes*."

"But I can't give you a firm *yes*."

Teresa drew in a deep breath. This was going to be an uphill battle all the way. "Can you at least give me a firm 'I'll try'?"

"I guess so."

Teresa released a sigh. No use pressing the child any further. She was giving all she could give. "Okay, here's what we're going to do. We're going to have a coaching session every day after school for the next three weeks."

Pilar's eyes widened. "Every day?"

"Yes, every day."

"But I can't come every day. I have volleyball practice after school—and homework."

Teresa considered. "Then how about three times a week? You can come on a Saturday for two sessions, if necessary."

Pilar didn't respond.

"Well?"

"I'll come on Saturdays if I have to."

"Let's plan for one session on Wednesday and two on Saturday for the next three weeks."

Pilar nodded without raising her eyes. "Are we finished for today?"

Teresa sighed. "Yes, we're finished for today." A sudden thought came to her. "Would you like to go clothes shopping with me tomorrow?"

Pilar gave her a strange look. "You want to go clothes shopping with *me*?"

"Yes." Teresa smiled. "You know the shops of Old San Juan better than I do. I could use your help to buy an outfit."

Pilar gave her a hint of a smile. "Okay. How about tomorrow?"

"Sounds great. Tomorrow is Saturday. I'll meet you in the lobby at ten. Then we'll take a cab into Old San Juan."

Pilar nodded in agreement. "I'll ask Papa, but I'm sure he won't mind."

Marcos wouldn't mind. He'd welcome the idea.

As Pilar left, Teresa reminded herself to ask Marcos if he'd spoken with his daughter about her mother's death.

Chapter Ten

Teresa found Pilar already in the lobby when she arrived at 9:55am. "*Hola*, early bird."

Pilar smiled. "Actually, I was afraid I'd be late. I got up only twenty minutes ago."

Teresa laughed, remembering her own teen years when she'd sleep till noon on Saturdays. "Our cab is waiting for us. Let's go." Teresa slung her purse over her shoulder and followed Pilar out to the waiting taxi cab. "Where are we going, my dear, young shopping partner?"

Pilar giggled. "Avenida Ashford. It's the heart of San Juan's shopping district."

Teresa repeated the address to the cab driver. Soon they arrived at the bustling center of the city's fashion district. High-end boutiques, including Louis Vuitton, Ferragamo, and Gucci, lined a street filled with tourists.

Teresa hooked her arm around Pilar's and smiled. "I'm depending on you to be my clothes coach today."

"Okay. If you don't find anything you like here, we could go to Calle Cristo. There are lots of factory outlets there that sell brand names at good prices."

"That sounds more like my style, but since we're here, let's check it out. If I find something I like, I may splurge."

They entered the Gucci store. Shelves of perfectly organized handbags lined one wall, while along another, racks of brightly colored, casual maxi-dresses invited closer exploration. Teresa approached the dress rack. "Your grandmother invited me to dinner at her apartment. Do you think one of these maxi-dresses would be appropriate for the event?"

"A maxi-dress always works well for evenings in Puerto Rico." Pilar stood by the rack. "I'm a jeans person myself, but I like maxi-dresses."

"Then let me buy one for you and we can both dress up. We'll surprise *Abuela* Ramona."

Pilar lowered her eyes. "You don't need to buy me anything. I'm just here to help."

"But I want to. Please let me. To thank you for helping me today." Teresa started looking through the rack. "What size do you wear?"

Pilar hesitated then spoke. "Junior, Size Five."

With Pilar at her side, Teresa located the Junior Size Five section. "When was the last time you went shopping for clothes?"

"Oh, I don't know. Maybe about two years ago. Papa is always too busy to take me shopping, and *Abuela* Ramona takes me whenever I outgrow my old clothes."

Teresa's heart clenched. Pilar needed a mother. Someone to make sure not only her physical needs were met but her emotional needs as well. She needed a mother to take her clothes shopping. To teach her how to put on makeup.

To help her grow into a Godly woman.

"Do you like this one?" Teresa pulled out a bright, lemon-colored dress with red hibiscus flowers painted all over it and held it up in front of Pilar.

"It's pretty, but I like this one better." Pilar lifted a hot pink dress from the rack. It had white butterflies embroidered on the bodice, while a single large white butterfly graced the hemline. She held it up to herself. "What do you think?"

"It's lovely. The hot pink looks great on you. Go try it on."

When Pilar emerged from the dressing room, Teresa

blinked back tears at the sight of this precious young girl on the cusp of womanhood. "You look beautiful! Wait till your Papa and *Abuela* Ramona see you in that dress."

Pilar fingered the soft fabric as she looked in the full-length mirror outside the dressing room. "Thank you, Teresa." Her voice cracked.

Teresa swallowed the lump in her throat. This was the first time she'd called Teresa by her first name. "You're welcome, Sweetheart."

"What about you?"

Teresa raised an eyebrow. "What do you mean?"

"What about a dress for you?"

In the joy of the moment, Teresa had completely forgotten her reason for being here. "Oh, yes." She chuckled. "A dress for me. Do you see any here that would look good on me? I wear a Misses Size Eight. "

Pilar walked over to the Misses Size Eight rack and looked through it. "Here. I think this one would be perfect for you." She removed a red chiffon maxi-dress from the rack. It had a square-cut bodice with wide shoulder straps. Large hibiscus flowers splashed brilliant patches of yellow over the entire dress.

"Wow! You like bright colors, don't you?"

Pilar smiled and nodded. "I think this would look beautiful on you."

"I'll go try it on."

A few moments later, Teresa stood in front of the full-length mirror. The sight took her breath away. "You have a gift for fashion, dear Pilar."

"I think I just know how to read people's hearts."

Her own heart warming, Teresa turned to face her. "That is a great gift. You certainly read my heart right. This dress is perfect for me."

Now, if only Teresa could read Pilar's heart just as perfectly.

* * *

Two days later, Marcos sat in his lounge chair, awaiting Pilar's return from grocery shopping with her grandmother. For the past several days, he'd been watching for the right moment to ask Pilar if she blamed herself for her mother's death. "Lord, give me the right words to say. Most of all, give me the right heart attitude."

The door latch clicked, and Pilar entered the apartment. "*Hola*, papa."

"*Hola*, honey. How did the shopping go?"

She threw her purse onto the sofa and sat down. "It went okay. *Abuela* Ramona always tries to make it fun for me. I don't have the heart to tell her grocery shopping is my least favorite thing in the universe."

He picked up on the opportunity to engage Pilar. "What is your most favorite thing in the universe?"

She tilted her head and twisted a strand of her long, light brown hair. "Oh, I don't know. Probably walking the beach."

"Yes, walking the beach is wonderful. Your mother and I used to do that frequently."

Pilar bit her lower lip. "When did you do that?"

"We started shortly after we first met. And we continued to walk the beach until you—." He stopped short, shuddering at his *faux pas* and not knowing what to say.

"You mean until I killed her."

Her words came crashing in on him, like a ruptured dam out of control, roaring toward the broken places of his soul.

He rose and went to his child. Taking her in his arms, he held her trembling body close to his heart. "Pilar. My precious Pilar. All this time you have been carrying this lie in your heart. And you have been carrying it alone."

"But it's true, papa. I did kill her."

He stroked her hair and pushed it back from her tear-stained face. "Why do you think you killed your mother?"

"Because she died while giving birth to me. If I hadn't been born, she wouldn't have died."

He pressed her head against his chest, praying for the right words to say. "Pilar, darling. I want you to listen to me and to listen to me very carefully. You did not kill your mother. It was not your fault she died while giving birth to you. You must believe that."

Pilar pulled back from her father's embrace. "How can you say that?" Her voice cracked and her eyes flooded with fresh tears.

Marcos ached. If only Teresa were here. She would know what to say. *Lord, help me.*

"Your mother died because of a long-standing high blood pressure problem that created a complication during your delivery."

"See, I told you. If I hadn't been born, she wouldn't have died." She wrenched free from him.

"Pilar, your mother's problem was not related to you. Sometimes in life things just happen that we have no control over."

"You had control over it, Papa. You should have never had me. I've done nothing but bring heartache to your life."

"Pilar—"

He stretched out his arms but watched helplessly as she ran out of the room.

His insides crashed. Was there any reaching his child? Would she forever blame herself for Marguerita's death?

Would his little girl ever find peace?

He sank into the sofa and buried his head in his hands. He would talk with Teresa at dinner. She would know what to do.

* * *

Dinner with Marcos had become a nightly event. At the end of each day, Teresa would meet him in the dining room at six o'clock for their daily discussion about Pilar's progress.

This evening, Teresa arrived with a heavy heart. She'd been working with Pilar for almost three weeks, with little progress.

Marcos greeted her with a smile. "So? How did it go today?"

Teresa sat down in the chair he'd pulled out for her. "Not good. I'm beginning to wonder if I'm the right person to help Pilar." She rested her elbows on the table. "I've been coaching her for almost three weeks, and she still blames herself for her mother's death. I was hoping to have made more progress by now."

"But we still have two more months."

She shook her head. "If I don't see results by the end of this week, I'm going to count my losses and go back home." She didn't dare tell him the other reason for her decision to return home. That he was growing on her, and growing to the point of no return.

After dinner, they took a walk to the beach. The full moon shone brightly over the Atlantic, casting streams of shimmering white light across its waters. Teresa pulled her shrug around her shoulders. "This is so beautiful."

"Not as beautiful as the woman walking beside me."

She swallowed hard.

Marcos took her gently by the shoulders and turned her toward him. "Teresa." He drew closer, the warmth of his breath barely brushing her cheek. "Teresa, I don't know how to say this. But I must say it. I've fallen in love with you."

Her mind reeled as the word *No* screamed through her consciousness. "No, Marcos. You can't fall in love with me. You must not. You must not because I already belong to another." She drew back from him and pressed her palm against her forehead. "And I can't fall in love with you either because . . . ."

She burst into tears.

He took her in his arms and finished the sentence for her. "Because you won't allow yourself to be set free to love again. You've chained yourself to Roberto. You aren't even giving yourself a chance with me."

Every muscle in her body stiffened. She pulled away from him. "How could you say such a thing? I have not chained myself to Roberto. I married him of my own free will."

"And you must let go of him of your own free will." Marcos lowered his voice. "Just as I had to let go of Marguerita."

"But, I can't. Don't you understand, I can't? I would be betraying him. He was my life."

Marcos raked his fingers through his hair. "Look! I'm not Roberto, okay? I never will be." He reached for her hand. "Nor do I ever want to be. But I can offer you a new love. A different love. A love that will never die."

She stood before him, tears streaming down her face. Guilt about Roberto wrapped itself around her like iron chains. What should she do? Should she betray the husband who had loved her with everything he had? Who had given her the greatest joy her life had known?

Who had been her every breath?

Marcos placed his hands on her shoulders. "Teresa, I love you. Plain and simple. The relationship you and I can have will be different from the one you had with Roberto and from the one I had with Marguerita. Our relationship doesn't diminish the ones we had with them, nor does it betray them. But they're both gone." He lowered his voice. "And we're still here."

He took both her hands and looked deep into her eyes. "You have a choice. Either you let go of the past, or you die there."

He let go of her hands, turned from her, and walked back to the inn.

A sob caught in her throat. Roberto was gone, and gone forever. She was clinging to a phantom. No, she was doing more than clinging to it. She had willingly chained herself to it.

She glanced back and saw Marcos disappear into the inn. She'd hurt him. Hurt him badly. Best to leave him to his own thoughts. For the time being anyway.

She gazed at the large expanse of water before her. The ocean at night was dark and brooding. Just like her heart.

She drew in a deep breath of the salt air. Tomorrow, she'd book a return flight to New Jersey.

Chapter Eleven

The next day, Teresa stood in the lobby, her bags packed for her return trip to the States. She tapped her toe on the ceramic tile as she waited impatiently for the taxi cab that would take her to the airport. Having said her good-byes to Ramona that morning, Teresa had asked the dear lady to convey Teresa's thanks and good wishes to Marcos and Pilar. After Marcos' declaration of love for her the night before, Teresa didn't trust her heart to stay strong in his presence.

She started as Marcos approached her, short of breath from running. "Teresa, what are you doing? Where are you going? Mamá told me you had checked out. Weren't you even going to say goodbye?" Intense sorrow etched his face.

"I asked your mother to say good-bye to you and Pilar for me."

Marcos pleaded with her. "Please come into my office. I must have a word with you."

"My cab will be here soon."

"Your cab can wait. I must talk with you."

Reluctantly, she followed him into a small private office behind the main office.

He closed the door and took her hands in his. "Teresa, what happened? Tell me. Why are you leaving so abruptly?"

She couldn't look him in the eye. "Marcos, I don't know what else to do. Despite my best efforts, Pilar hasn't responded to my coaching." She couldn't bear to tell him she'd fallen in love with him and her heart was breaking at the thought of leaving him. But she had to leave to be faithful to Roberto.

Marcos squeezed her hands. "Don't berate yourself. It's not as if you didn't try."

"But trying isn't enough. Succeeding is what matters."

"You're really hard on yourself, aren't you?" His voice was tender. "Why?"

She pondered his question a long moment. "Maybe it's that I've had to succeed in order to survive. Since Roberto died, I've had to depend on myself to make it."

"Perhaps it's time you stop depending on yourself so much."

She stiffened. "What do you mean? I can take care of myself perfectly well, thank you."

"Well, you don't seem to be doing a very good job of it."

"How dare—"

He drew her close to his heart and pressed her head into his shoulder.

To her dismay, she did not resist.

"Teresa, please don't go. I can't bear to live without you."

The honking horn of the taxi cab disrupted the tender moment. She raised her head. "I must go, Marcos. My cab is waiting."

She turned and fled toward the waiting cab as hot tears rolled down her cheeks.

* * *

Teresa's plane touched down at Newark Airport and proceeded to the landing gate. Outside, a dreary rain pelted the aircraft like a million annoying pinpricks.

"Welcome to Newark." The captain's voice sounded over the intercom system. "Temperature 28 degrees, heavy rain expected to turn to snow this evening.

92

Thank you for flying Coastal Airlines."

Teresa gathered her carry-on case and proceeded down the aisle to exit the aircraft. What a contrast from beautiful, sunny Puerto Rico!

She found Mamá waiting for her in the arrivals area.

"Teresita, my precious Teresita! Welcome home." Mamá enveloped her in a tight embrace that threatened to empty Teresa of the little life remaining within her.

"*Hola*, Mamá. It's so good to see you."

Teresa locked arms with her mother, and the two proceeded toward baggage claim to pick up Teresa's luggage.

Mamá squeezed Teresa's arm. "It's so good to have you home."

"It's good to be home." The lump in her throat belied the words she spoke.

"But you really wish you were back in San Juan, don't you?"

The lump broke into a sob. Teresa stopped walking and buried her face in Mamá's winter coat. "Oh, Mamá. I'm so miserable."

Mamá patted her on the back. "Now, now. Ramona told me all about it."

Teresa raised her head and looked at Mamá. "Ramona?"

"Yes. Right after you left, she called me. She said Marcos is miserable and beside himself that you left." Mamá took a tissue from her purse and wiped Teresa's eyes. "Let's get your luggage and then stop for a cup of coffee before going home."

Her head spinning, Teresa dutifully followed Mamá to baggage claim then to the airport café where Mamá ordered two cups of black coffee.

Teresa blew her nose. "I need strong coffee right about now. I can't think straight."

"You can't think straight because your heart is

broken." Mamá took Teresa's hands. "Teresa, Marcos is in love with you. But not only is he in love with you, you are in love with him."

Teresa's stomach tightened. "I am not in love with Marcos. I am in love with Roberto."

Mamá's voice grew firm. "Teresa, you cannot be in love with a dead man. What you love is the memory of Roberto. And you can continue to love his memory. You had a good marriage. But you must let it go and move on with your life. Marcos is offering you a new life. Don't refuse it. It is a gift from God to you."

A gift from God. Was Mamá right? Was God really offering her a gift in Marcos?

"I'm tired, Mamá. Maybe we can talk about this after I get some rest, okay?"

Mamá nodded. "All right. I understand. How did things go with Pilar?"

"Awful. The girl never warmed up to me. She didn't want to be coached, so there wasn't much I could do to help her. Each session was like pulling teeth."

"I'm sorry to hear that."

"I feel as though the whole trip was a waste of time."

"You must have made some impression on the child."

"Yes. Enough for her to be glad I left, I'm sure."

"Teresa, don't be so hard on yourself."

"That's exactly what Marcos said."

Mama smiled. "I thought you didn't want to talk about Marcos."

Teresa's muscles tensed. "Let's go, Mamá. I really want to get home."

"Home is where your heart is."

Teresa's throat constricted. Where was her heart? Really?

If she were brutally honest with herself, she had to

admit she'd left her heart with Marcos in Old San Juan.

* * *

Two weeks later, on a dreary Valentine's Day, Teresa visited Roberto's grave. Being back in New Jersey had given her a semblance of equilibrium, but still her heart longed for Marcos. She hadn't heard from him since her departure. Nor, truth be told, had she expected to. Upon leaving she'd made it quite clear she wasn't interested in a relationship with him. Not now. Not ever.

During her absence, weeds had grown over Roberto's gravesite. She knelt in front of the headstone and began pulling them out one by one. Tears spilled from her eyes as she prayed. "Father, how can I go on without Roberto, my very life?"

I am your Life, dear one.

"Lord, why can't I let him go?"

You are afraid.

"Afraid of what?"

Afraid of loving again.

The Lord's words surprised her. "Afraid of loving again?"

Yes, dear one. Loving Roberto brought great pain when he died. And you do not want to experience ever again the pain that love can bring.

Teresa pondered the Lord's words. *The pain that love can bring.* "Lord, can there be love without pain?"

No, dear one. Just look at the Cross.

Revelation pierced her heart. It was clear now. The Cross represented Christ's surrender to love. A love that caused Him the greatest pain of all. If she wanted to be like Him, she, too, must surrender to the pain of love.

"O, God, forgive me! Forgive me for refusing to love." She stood and looked heavenward as the sun burst forth from behind gray clouds. "I haven't been guarding my faithfulness to Roberto at all. I've been protecting myself from the pain of loving again."

Yes, Teresa. Now you see. Love requires willing surrender to pain. But that very surrender to pain leads to the joy of new life.

She took a tissue from her purse and dried her eyes. Then she started to laugh. "Lord, You should be a life coach."

In the depths of her spirit, she heard God's laughter in response.

She looked one last time at Roberto's grave. He was with the Lord, enjoying eternal life. She was still on earth and would enjoy earthly life as long as God kept her here.

The clouds of deception rolled away from her soul.

She looked down at the grave. "Goodbye, Roberto."

Then turning away, she walked into the peace of whatever future God had for her.

Chapter Twelve

It was noon when Teresa arrived home. The aroma of homemade chili caught her nostrils as she walked in the kitchen door. "*Hola*, Mamá. Mmm. Something smells good."

Mamá smiled, a twinkle in her eye.

Teresa walked over to the stove and lifted the lid. "Wow! You've made enough for an army."

Mamá hugged Teresa then motioned with a tilt of her head toward the living room. "There's someone here to see you."

Teresa furrowed her brows. "To see *me*?"

Mamá nodded, a mischievous smile on her lips.

What was going on? Teresa walked toward the living room. As she crossed the threshold, her heart stopped. There before her stood Marcos and Pilar. Huge smiles brightened their faces.

"Marcos! Pilar! What are you doing here?"

Marcos stepped forward. "Teresa, I hope you're not angry. We could not stay away. We could not let you go."

"We?"

Pilar drew near her and took her by the arm. "I'm sorry for making you leave, Teresa. Will you come back to Puerto Rico with us?"

Teresa's body trembled. "But I thought you didn't want a life coach."

"I don't." Pilar giggled. "I want a mother."

Teresa's head spun as she looked questioningly at Marcos through tear-filled eyes.

He stroked her cheek. "I'll ask you again, Teresa. Will you marry me?"

Pilar tugged on her arm. "Please say *yes*. Please say *yes*."

Teresa turned toward Mamá who had entered the room. The older woman's face beamed with total approval.

Teresa's heart clenched.

Dear one, I have not given you a spirit of fear, but a spirit of love."

This time she resisted the fear that tried yet again to keep her from surrendering to love.

She inhaled a deep breath. She smiled and looked deep into Marcos' eyes. "Yes, Marcos, I will marry you."

He drew her into his embrace.

Teresa then turned to Pilar and smiled. "And yes, Pilar, I will be your mother."

"Yay!" Pilar jumped up and down then threw her arms around Teresa's neck.

Mamá clapped her hands in delight. *"Gracias, Señor!* Thank You, Lord!" Mamá joined her hug to the huddle. "We must start making wedding plans right away."

Teresa laughed. "Mamá, this is your big chance to visit your homeland."

"You mean the wedding will be in Puerto Rico?"

"Yes, the wedding will be in Puerto Rico." Teresa set her gaze on Marcos. "As will my new life with Marcos and Pilar."

* * *

The first of May in Old San Juan brought with it a taste of heaven. A cloudless blue sky formed a majestic mantle over a day that was perfect in every way.

Escorted by Uncle Miguel, her mother's brother, and attended to by Pilar, her maid of honor, Teresa walked slowly down the red carpet spread out on the beach in front of the *Inn of the Dove*. Ramona and Mamá stood watching in the front row, arms clasped and faces beaming with joy.

At the end of the carpet, just in front of a large wooden Cross, stood Marcos in a white tuxedo with a red rose in his lapel. A smile as wide as the ocean adorned his gentle face.

At the sight of him, Teresa's heart beat in rhythm with the pounding waves. Before her, the shimmering Atlantic lay in all of its magnificent expanse.

Suddenly, from the crest of one of its foamy waves, a seagull soared toward the heavens. Teresa's heart soared with it.

Soar, My beloved. Soar into the destiny for which I have created you. Behold, I make all things new. Surrender to My love and you shall surely live.

Teresa laughed. "I surrender, Lord. I surrender."

Discussion Questions for Groups

1. Teresa struggles greatly to deal with the grief that follows her husband's death. In fact, she struggles so much that even after five years, she cannot move on with her life. Have you ever suffered with deep grief? How did you handle it? Does God offer insight in His Word as to how to handle grief?

2. Marcos is a man of prayer who is having serious challenges being a single father. What are some of the challenges that single parents face? How can you, as a follower of Jesus, help a parent who is raising a child alone? Perhaps you are that parent. What kind of help would you appreciate from others in the Body of Christ?

3. Teresa learns at the end that fear of pain kept her from moving on with her life. Have you ever been so afraid that you became emotionally paralyzed? What did you do? What does God have to say about fear in His Word?

4. Pilar blames herself for her mother's death by believing a lie. What lies have you believed that have caused you unnecessary anguish? Jesus said that knowing the truth will set us free (John 8:32). Why does knowing the truth make us free? How can we know the truth?

5. Marisol wants what is best for her daughter Teresa, but sometimes Marisol can be overbearing. How can we influence our children without interfering with their free wills?

6. What does it mean to surrender to Christ? Can you give examples in your life when you have surrendered to Christ? What were the consequences? Can you give

examples in your life when you did not surrender to Christ? What were the consequences?

7. What does it mean to surrender to love? Is it true that loving involves pain? What can one do if she is afraid of the pain that loving may bring? What does the Cross have to say about the pain of loving?

8. What role does surrender play in the life of a follower of Jesus? Why is it that many Christians are afraid to surrender? What is it that one surrenders when one follows Jesus?

9. What did you learn from reading this story? Was there one thing that touched your heart in a special way?

10. Did this story make you think about your life in a new way? Did it make you think about Jesus in a new way?

How to Live Forever

Eternal life is a free gift offered by God to anyone who chooses to accept it. All it takes is a sincere sorrow for your sins (contrition) and a quality decision to turn away from your sins (repentance) and begin living for God.

In John 3:3, Jesus said, "Unless a man is born again, he cannot see the Kingdom of God." What does it mean to be "born again?" Simply put, it means to be restored to fellowship with God.

Man is made up of three parts: spirit, soul, and body (I Thessalonians 5:23). Your spirit is who you really are; your soul is comprised of your mind, your will, and your emotions; and your body is the housing for your spirit and your soul. You could call your body your "earth suit."

When we are born into this world, we are born with a spirit that is separated from God. As a result, it is a spirit without life because God alone is the Source of life. You may have heard this condition referred to as "original sin." Why is every human being born with a spirit separated from God? Because of the sin of our first parents, Adam and Eve.

I used to wonder why I had to suffer because of the sin of Adam and Eve. After all, I complained, I wasn't even there when they ate the apple! Yet, as I began to understand spiritual matters, I began to see that I was there just as a man and woman's children, grandchildren, great-grandchildren, and so on, are in the body of the man and woman in seed form before those descendants are actually born. In other words, in my children there is already the seed for their future children. In their future children will be the seed of their future children, and so on.

Now, as a parent, I can pass on to my children only what I am and what I possess. For example, if I speak only Chinese, I can pass on to my children only the Chinese language. I possess no other language to give them out of my own self. The same was true with Adam and Eve. Because they disobeyed God, their fellowship with God was broken. Therefore, their spirits died because they were severed from God. As a result, they could pass on to their children only a dead spirit—a sinful spirit separated from God. And Adam and Eve's children could pass on to their children only a dead, sinful spirit. And so on, all the way down to you and me.

We said earlier that your spirit is the real you—who you really are. So what does it mean when your spirit—the real you—is separated from God? It means that unless you are somehow reconciled to God, you will go to hell after you die. Hell is a real place of real torment resulting from separation from God.

Now God is a holy God and He will not tolerate sin in His Presence. At the same time, He is a loving God. Indeed, He IS Love! And because He loves you so much, He wanted to restore the broken relationship between you and Himself. He wanted to restore you to that glorious position of walking and talking with Him and enjoying the fullness of His blessings.

But there was a problem. Because God is infinite, only an infinite Being could satisfy the price of man's offense against God. At the same time, because man committed the offense, there had to be Someone Who would also be able to represent man in paying this price. In other words, there had to be a Being Who was both God and man in order that the price for sin could be paid.

Since God knew that there was nothing man could do on his own to pay the price for his sin, God took the initiative. In the writings of John the Apostle, we learn that "God so loved the world that He gave His only-begotten Son, that whoever believes in Him shall not perish but have eternal life" (John 3:16).

What glorious GOOD NEWS! God loved you so much that He sent His own and only Son, Jesus Christ, to take the rap for your sins. Imagine that! Would you give your son to go to the electric chair for someone else? Well, that's exactly what God did! The Cross was the electric chair of Christ's day, and God gave His own Son, Jesus Christ, to go to the Cross for you!

In dying on the Cross for you, and in rising from the dead three days later, Jesus paid the price for your sins and repaired the breach between you and God the Father. Jesus restored the broken relationship between man and God. He provided mankind with the gift of eternal life.

So what does all of this mean for you? It means that if you accept Christ's gift of eternal life, you will be "born again." In other words, God will replace your dead spirit with a spirit filled with His life. "Therefore, if anyone is in Christ, he is a new creation. Old things have passed away; behold, all things have become new" (2 Corinthians 5:17).

If I offer you a gift, it is not yours until you choose to take it. The same is true with the gift of eternal life. Until you choose to take it, it is not yours. In order for you to be born again, you must reach out and take the gift of eternal life that Jesus is offering you now. Here is how to receive it:

"Lord Jesus, I come to You now just as I am—broken, bruised, and empty inside. I've made a mess of my life, and I need You to fix it. Please forgive me of all of my sins. I accept You now as my personal Savior and as the Lord of my life. Thank You for dying for me so that I might live. As I give you my life, I trust that You will make of me all that You've created me to be. Amen."

If you prayed this prayer, please write to me to let me know. You may reach me at drmaryann@maryanndiorio.com. I will send you some information to help you get started in your Christian walk. Also, I encourage you to do three important things:

1) Get yourself a Bible and begin reading in the Gospel of John.
2) Find yourself a good church that preaches the full Gospel. Ask God to lead you to a church where you will be fed.
3) Set aside a time every day for prayer. Prayer is simply talking to God as you would to your best friend.

I congratulate you on making the life-changing decision to accept Jesus Christ! It is the most important decision of your life. Mark down this date because it is the date of your spiritual birthday. Be assured of my prayers for you as you grow in your Christian walk. God bless you!

About the Author

MaryAnn Diorio's passion, as her registered trademark states, is to proclaim *Truth through Fiction*® because only truth will set people free (John 8:32). A widely published author of non-fiction, MaryAnn responded to God's call a few years ago to write fiction and has since published one novella for adults, A CHRISTMAS HOMECOMING, and a chapter book for 8-12 year-old children, DO ANGELS RIDE PONIES? She hopes her stories will entertain and point readers to Jesus Christ, the Truth Who alone can set them free.

Dr. MaryAnn holds the PhD in French and Comparative Literature, the MFA in Writing Popular Fiction, and the DMin in Christian Counseling. She lives in New Jersey with her husband Dominic, a physician. They are blessed with two lovely grown daughters, a wonderful son-in-law, and five rambunctious grandchildren. In her spare time, MaryAnn loves to read, paint, and make up silly songs for her grandchildren.

Other Books by MaryAnn Diorio

A CHRISTMAS HOMECOMING (Novella)
Winner of 2015 Illumination Book Award for E-Book Fiction

DO ANGELS RIDE PONIES? (Children's Chapter Book)

YOU WERE MADE FOR GREATNESS!

WHO IS JESUS? (Children's Picture Book)
Finalist in 2015 National Indie Book Awards Contest

GOD SPEAKS TO ME: TWO-WAY CONVERSATIONS
WITH GOD

MATTERS OF THE HEART (Dr. MaryAnn's Blog)
To sign up for *Matters of the Heart*, please click here or go to

http://www.networkedblogs.com/blog/maryanndmarioblog

To subscribe to Dr. MaryAnn's quarterly newsletter, please
click here or go to

http://visitor.constantcontact.com/manage/optin?v=001sWE8kxl
6JoloLv4gPxbZoXetjtz7GCRJ5hHxZwWX0ZUvdxsivc5LUU5l
OMfh1KiUknVzs6l-uCFZIkMOdWsUCX_ELVk08lNq

Dr. MaryAnn's Social Media Venues

Website: www.maryanndiorio.com
 Blog (Matters of the Heart):
http://www.networkedblogs.com/blog/maryanndmarioblog
Amazon Author Central: www.amazon.com/author/maryanndiorio
Facebook: www.Facebook.com/DrMaryAnnDiorio
Goodreads:
https://www.goodreads.com/author/show/6592603.MaryAnn_Diorio
LinkedIn: https://www.linkedin.com/profile/view?id=45380421
Pinterest: https://www.pinterest.com/drmaryanndiorio/
Google+: https://plus.google.com/u/0/+DrMaryAnnDiorio/posts
YouTube: https://www.youtube.com/user/drmaryanndiorio/

Excerpt from A CHRISTMAS HOMECOMING:

Sonia put the finishing touches on the German chocolate cake she'd baked for Christmas Eve dinner. If Ben didn't want to join her, she'd take the cake to old Miss Hattie, a shut-in who lived next door, and share it with her.

As Christmas carols played softly in the background, Sonia sang along with Silver Bells, hoping to put herself in the Christmas spirit. A ring of what sounded like the doorbell interrupted her. No. It must be the sound of bells on the CD. It sounded again, but she ignored it a second time. But when the ring sounded a third time, she turned off the CD to listen. Yes, it was the doorbell.

She carefully put down the frosting-laden spatula and wiped her hands on a kitchen towel. Then she hurried to answer the front door. Probably the mail carrier or the FedEx man. Who else could it be? She wasn't expecting anyone, especially not on Christmas Eve.

She reached for the door knob and opened the door. Her heart froze at the sight before her.

Purchase your copy here.

Excerpt from DO ANGELS RIDE PONIES?

Jeremiah took a deep breath. Leaning forward, he grabbed the stall gate with both hands and began to pull himself up. It took every ounce of strength he could muster to raise his crippled body.

Thunder began to neigh and move about.

"Hold still, Thunder," Jeremiah shouted.

Jeremiah pushed himself up, his hands gripping the gate. Beneath him, his legs felt like jelly. If he didn't grab Thunder's neck soon, he would surely fall back into his wheelchair.

Releasing one hand, Jeremiah reached forward to grab the palomino's thick mane, but Thunder moved away. Jeremiah felt his legs beginning to give way. But then he remembered Jake's words: *All things are possible to him who believes.*

Once again, Jeremiah reached for Thunder's mane. "Almost there," he said.

But just as he was about to grab the pony's neck, he fell forward and went crashing into the stall.

Frightened by the fall, Thunder reared back, neighing wildly.

Jeremiah panicked as he lay helpless on the ground.

Purchase your copy here.

TopNotch Press

A Division of MaryAnn Diorio Enterprises, LLC
PO Box 1185
Merchantville, NJ 08109
Tel.: 856-488-3580
FAX: 856-488-0291
Email: info@maryanndiorio.com

www.ingramcontent.com/pod-product-compliance
Lightning Source LLC
Chambersburg PA
CBHW071133250626
47159CB00006B/2219